HONEY FOR TEA

*Also by Elizabeth Cadell
in Thorndike Large Print*

THE GOLDEN COLLAR
THE CUCKOO IN SPRING

Honey for Tea

ELIZABETH CADELL

THORNDIKE PRESS • THORNDIKE, MAINE

Library of Congress Cataloging in Publication Data

Cadell, Elizabeth.
  Honey for tea.

  Originally published: New York : Morrow, 1962,
c1961.
  1. Large type books. I. Title.
[PR6005.A225H6   1985]   823'.912   85–2589
ISBN 0–89621–618–7 (lg. print)

Large Print edition available through arrangement with
Brandt and Brandt Literary Agents, Inc., New York.

Cover design by Holly Hughes

HONEY FOR TEA

CHAPTER 1

Jendy Marsh was smiling as she emerged from the scarlet door of her Mews flat and walked to the adjoining garage. The smile persisted as she backed her small, shabby car out onto the cobbled yard and drove it out into the street. Then, with an effort, she assumed what she called a London expression — by which she meant no expression at all. But before she had driven far, the smile had returned.

Why, she asked herself as she slid neatly between two buses and listened with detachment to the comments of the drivers, why should she feel so elated merely because she was on her way to Waterloo Station to meet her sister? Surely a sister — a sister, moreover, she had seen less than four months ago — didn't rate this upsurge of excitement?

Yes. Nancy, she decided, edging past a

Rolls-Royce at the traffic lights, wasn't like other people's sisters. Nancy was . . . well, she was Nancy; gay, amusing, warm-hearted, generous. And beautiful to boot.

Nancy, who was three years older than herself, but who had been too sensible to settle down in a cramped London flat with no view except the spike-topped wall surrounding Buckingham Palace; who had elected to stay at home at Tallahouse, painting, gardening, helping Aunt Eddie to look after the house — a house that offered little in the way of modern comforts, but which was admitted to be one of the most beautiful old buildings in England.

And then, two years ago, Nancy had gone in search of warmth and color and had found them in a studio in Madrid. She had lived there for a year and eight months, and had then returned to England, to Tallahouse and to thirty-four-year-old Allen Harvey, a neighboring farmer who had known her all her life and had loved her almost as long.

And in less than six weeks, Jendy remembered with feelings equally balanced between pain and pleasure, she would marry Allen and live at Farhills Farm and have children as beautiful as herself or as handsome as Allen.

Nancy and Allen . . . and their family . . .

She came back to the present to realize that in the excitement caused by Nancy's unexpected telephone call that morning asking her to meet her, she had forgotten to inform her employer that she would be unable to go to work that day. She was a free-lance secretary. After spending some time in an office and discovering that she disliked the dull routine, that she was an exceptionally efficient worker and that she could earn almost as much by taking a series of temporary jobs, she had put herself on the books of a local agency, and since then had never had a workless day — unless she chose to. She had enough money of her own to take the edge off the necessity of earning her own living; she could afford to run a small car, and she was able to enjoy the luxury of living alone.

She parked the car at Waterloo station and walked across to the telephones. As she crossed the yard, a spatter of rain fell, giving way almost at once to a burst of sunshine and making her feel that April was the best month of all: a clean month, with winds that blew away the heaviness of winter and brought a promise of lovely days to come.

She shut herself into a booth, dialed a number and heard the voice of her employer, a seventy-year-old author who sounded disappointed at Jendy's inability to work that day, but who expressed his willingness to wait until she could be with him again.

"Nobody," he said with gratifying sincerity, "has ever done my work so well before. Why can't you come today?"

"My sister is coming up to town; she rang up this morning to ask me to meet her train."

"Your sister . . . she's getting married, isn't she?"

"Yes."

"I suppose you're going on a buying spree?"

"She didn't say why she was coming, but I imagine that's what the reason will be."

"Well, don't spend all your money. Who's she marrying?"

Jendy told him, put the receiver down and went out of the phone booth wondering what her listener's reactions would have been if she had told him the truth: that Nancy was marrying the man she herself loved.

If you couldn't cure something, she mused, walking into the noisy, echoing station, you had to learn to live with it. That was what

10

she had done with this thing called love: she had learned to live with it. There had been plenty of time in which to learn. She made a grim calculation: she was twenty-four, and she had fallen in love with Allen Harvey, and with his home, Farhills Farm, when she was seventeen. Seventeen from twenty-four was time enough, indeed.

A picture of Farhills came to her mind, springing green and lovely from the gloom of the station. The farm spread over nine hundred picturesque and productive acres. The farmhouse was sheltered: a long, low, lovely old building set a little way up a hill, with a view of the red, rolling Devonshire country and the sea beyond. Inside, the house was lowbeamed, dark in a restful and not at all depressing way, full of furniture that nobody for generations had changed: gleaming, like the floors; an integral part of the room, like the fine old rugs. Allen Harvey's house; his father's and grandfather's and great-grandfather's before him. As unmistakably a man's house, as Tallahouse had always been a woman's. Jendy, watching the picture fade, felt with a tightening of her throat that she would have given half her life to have lived the other half at Farhills — with Allen.

But Allen had never looked at anybody but Nancy. He had loved her for years, waited for her for years. Unable to dissuade her from going to Spain, he had waited for her to return to him. And she had returned four months ago, and soon the years of waiting would be at an end and Nancy would be his wife.

Jendy shook herself out of her depression and made her way to the arrivals board, standing before it and disentangling times and trains and platforms. And then she heard Nancy's voice.

"Hello, Jendy."

She swung around, but it was impossible to return the greeting. Two engines had begun to let off steam with long, vindictive hisses. A third, apparently in the hands of a learner-driver, was starting on its journey with a series of convulsive jerks. Another, having discharged its passengers, was backing out of the station with the swift puff-puff-puff of nursery models. All Jendy could do was take one of the small cases that Nancy was carrying, and turn her in the direction of the parking lot.

They walked toward it, sometimes together, sometimes separated by the rush of people hurrying toward the trains; even in

April and even so early on a Friday afternoon, there seemed to be a steady flow out of town. One or two heads turned as they passed, to catch another glimpse of the tall, beautiful, beautifully-dressed dark young woman, or the shorter, slighter, younger and fairer one.

It was not until they were in the car and Jendy had switched on the engine that she realized that Nancy seemed oddly silent.

"Tired?" she asked.

"No. Yes. I want a drink."

"At two-thirty in the afternoon? Didn't you have lunch on the train?"

"No. Don't you read the papers? The restaurant-car waiters are on strike. I bought sandwiches at one station and a bottle of milk at another."

Something in the tone — brusque, almost sharp, and totally unlike Nancy's usual calm, slow speech — told Jendy that something was badly wrong. And with the realization came wonder that she had not sensed trouble before. Many things could have, should have warned her: why, in the first place, would Nancy have come up by train? If she had wanted to come to London, Allen would have driven her up. Why should she have telephoned at a — for Nancy — phenomenally early hour to say she was arriving just after lunch? And why hadn't she come on the train she had stated she was coming on? Jendy had had time to note that it was not yet due but the sound of Nancy's voice had driven the fact from her mind. And finally, why was Nancy carrying the handbag she only used when she was going away? — the bag which had pockets for her passport, her air ticket, her travelers' checks . . . Why . . .

She drove slowly out of the station yard.

"There's something wrong," she said.

"Yes." Nancy's voice was quiet. "Don't talk about it until we get to the flat."

There was silence until Jendy stopped the car at the scarlet door. Still silent, they walked up the steep, narrow staircase and crossed the tiny hall at the top. When they entered the little living room, a sudden feeling of fear or depression made Jendy walk to one of the windows and throw it open. Then she turned and looked at Nancy.

"What is it?" she asked.

Nancy opened her bag, took out a cigarette and lit it, and Jendy saw with horror that her hands were shaking.

"Nancy, what is it . . . ?"

"I'm going away," Nancy said quietly.

"Away?" Jendy's tone was blank.

14

"Yes."

"Away where? When? Why?"

"I'm going back to Spain."

For some moments, Jendy could only stare stupidly at her.

"When?" she brought out at last. "For how long?"

"I'm not coming back."

There was a long silence. At last Jendy broke it.

"I don't understand," she said slowly. "In six weeks' time, you're going to marry Allen."

"No, I'm not," said Nancy.

Jendy stared at her, struggling to speak. "You're . . . you're . . ."

"I'm not going to marry Allen, Jendy." Nancy spoke without emphasis. "I thought I could. I came back to England because I thought I could. But I find I can't. I've been fighting for the past weeks to come to a decision — and I've come to one. I'm not going to marry him. I'm going back to Spain."

"I'm being stupid." Jendy spoke carefully at the end of another long silence. "I just don't understand what you mean. You came back here to —"

"— marry Allen. Quite true. And I became

engaged to him and —"

"You've had a quarrel?"

"No. We didn't quarrel. I told him I couldn't marry him."

"You told him . . . When?"

"Last night."

"You . . . What did you say to him?"

"I told him the truth. At least, I told him most of it. I told him I couldn't live his life. I told him that I can't, don't want to . . . *won't* stay in England. I want to live abroad — in Spain. I don't want to be a farmer's wife and live for the rest of my life on a Devonshire farm seeing nobody, doing nothing but the routine things farmers' wives have to do, seeing year after agricultural year come and go and . . . I can't do it, Jendy, I can't — and I won't."

"You . . . you told him that?"

"Yes. I needn't have said it all. He knew most of it. He's suspected it ever since I came back. I was a fool to think I could give up the kind of life I love, the —"

"What kind of life?" broke in Jendy.

"Life with movement and color. Life in the sun. Life in a country where —"

"You were born and brought up in this country. You're English. You're not Spanish, and you can't —"

16

"I'm twenty-seven, and that makes me old enough to decide what I want."

"And what do you want? Life in a studio in a street in Madrid?"

"Why not?"

"Why? Because you can't give up your own country — and a man like Allen — just because you enjoyed spending a year or so among foreigners. You don't throw away the chance of living with Allen for a —"

"I've told you, and I've told Allen and I've told Aunt Eddie: I can't marry him. I should never have come back."

"Then why did you?" Jendy asked passionately. "Why did you come back, get engaged to him, make plans to marry him, let him believe that after years of keeping him on a string, you'd at last realized how lucky you were to have the chance of marrying a man like him? Why did you do it? Why?"

"I've told you why."

"No, you haven't. All you've told me is that Spain's a colorful country, which I knew already. If it meant all that to you, why didn't you stay there and spare Allen all this . . . this . . ."

"I shouldn't have come back. But I told myself all the things you're trying to tell me:

that I belonged here, that Allen was a man in a million, that being in love with Spain was a passing phase, that . . . Well, I came back. I came back meaning to settle down, marry Allen and live for the rest of my life at Farhills. And now I know I can't — and that's all."

"All? You break a man's heart, and you say that's all?"

She saw Nancy turn pale, and realized that for the first time in their lives she was looking at her with something less than affection. They stood in silence for some moments.

"When did you tell Aunt Eddie?" Jendy asked quietly at last.

"Last night."

"What did she say?"

"She said I was out of my mind."

"That's what I think, too. I think . . ."

She made a strong effort to control the anger that was choking her. Her mind was confused, but one conclusion emerged clearly enough: it was one thing to stand aside and watch another woman making the man she loved happy — but it was quite another to see her throwing his patience, his gentleness and understanding back in his face. She had told Nancy that she thought that she was crazy, and at that moment she almost believed it. No sane woman could throw away so much — for so little. But that was what Nancy was doing. She was giving up Allen, giving up life at Farhills and going away to live in a foreign country. And Allen . . . Allen was thirty-four. A man of thirty-four would not get over it as one of twenty-four might have done.

She felt that it would be safer for the moment to say nothing more. She went into the kitchen and began to make coffee. She did not want coffee and she did not think that Nancy wanted it either, but she felt some of the blind anger draining from her as she worked.

On previous visits, Nancy had always followed her out to the kitchen; she gave no practical assistance, but she talked, and to Jendy it had always seemed like working to music. Today, Nancy stayed in the living room. When Jendy carried in the coffee, she was standing by the window, staring out unseeingly.

"Sit down," Jendy said. "We'd better talk this over quietly. And drink something; you look terrible."

Nancy sat on the sofa, holding her cup in her hands as though she needed to warm them.

"There's nothing more to say, Jendy. I've said that I'm going and you've said I'm crazy, and you're right. But I've talked to myself — out loud — for weeks, and I'm tired of talking. Telling myself that Allen loves me and that I ought to marry him and make him a good wife doesn't make me feel that I can do it."

"Don't you love him?"

"Yes."

The answer came without hesitation, and with complete assurance. It was impossible to doubt its sincerity.

"But if you love him," began Jendy in bewilderment, "you —"

"Try to understand. Aunt Eddie didn't — or wouldn't. Before I came back to England four months ago, I made myself believe that everything would work out. It hasn't. It doesn't. It won't. I came back and I got engaged to Allen, and I began to realize that I'd made a mistake. And so I wrote and asked you to come home. I thought that if you were there, I might have worked things out your way, instead of my way. We could have talked . . . Why didn't you come, Jendy?"

It was not possible to tell her why. Going

home was something that Jendy had done as little as possible during the past few years. Going home had meant seeing Allen — and she had felt that her best chance of happiness lay in not seeing Allen. Her greatest comfort had come from the certainty that neither he nor Nancy had the least suspicion of her feelings toward him. Even Aunt Eddie's sharp nose had smelled out nothing. But she had felt that it was safer to stay away. She had gone home at Christmas and at Easter, and sometimes for Aunt Eddie's birthday or her own — but she had stayed only a few days, and she had been glad to return to London. Much as she longed to spend long days wandering around Farhills, as she and Nancy had done all their lives, she had felt it wiser to keep away.

"What did Allen say when you told him?" she asked.

"Nothing much." Nancy stared at the steaming cup as though she saw his face there. "He listened and he . . . he made it very easy for me." A tear trickled down her cheek, and then another and another, but the sight, which yesterday would have sent Jendy rushing across to comfort her, today left her unmoved. "He said he understood, and he said he'd . . . he'd seen it coming.

He drove me back to Tallahouse and took me inside to tell Aunt Eddie." She was speaking in a monotone, making no attempt to stem the tears that poured down her face. "Aunt Eddie just sat there looking like stone, and Allen said that it would be better if I packed straightaway and left first thing this morning. I was going to ring you up last night, but once Allen had gone, I couldn't bear the look on Aunt Eddie's face, and I went upstairs and stayed in my room and didn't come down again. Allen drove me to the station this morning, but I came up on an earlier train because I wanted to put my heavy luggage out of sight before you arrived. If you'd seen it, you would have asked questions at once, and I couldn't have borne that."

"You don't mean that you meant to go at once? Today?"

"No. I . . . I'd like to stay for a day or two. If you'll let me. Not to talk; not to argue. Just to be with you for a little while to . . . to get my bearings."

She stayed for three days, and though during that time Jendy made several attempts to persuade her to return to Allen, she did not press her too far. Something about Nancy's face and manner frightened her; she looked like a woman who had taken as much as she could stand.

"Will you go down and stay with Aunt Eddie when I've gone?" she begged Jendy.

Jendy hesitated.

"I don't want to. I've got my job up here. And I've never got on as well with Aunt Eddie as you have."

"I wish you'd go. This has . . . it's hurt her badly."

"Why wouldn't it hurt her? Seeing you married to Allen was something she set her heart on years and years ago. Her godson — and her favorite niece. Why wouldn't she be hurt?"

"You could go down there for a little while. It would help her — and Allen."

"Nobody can do anything for Allen."

"You can talk to him. You can make it easier for him."

Jendy stared at her.

"You really know what you're doing?" she asked slowly.

"Yes, I know. Other women have discovered that they couldn't marry a man even —"

"— even if they loved and were loved? The men couldn't have been like Allen."

Allen. Big, safe, kind, patient,

gentle, strong . . .

Jendy rose and took the tray back to the kitchen, and this time Nancy followed her and stood watching as she washed and stacked the cups.

"Will you go, Jendy?" she asked.

Jendy turned and looked at her, and suddenly it was borne upon her that this was really true. It was settled. It was over. Nancy was really going. She was going, and in the future, if Jendy wanted to see her, she would have to go to Madrid and see her there. Their lives would lie apart. There would be no happy home to visit at Farhills, no children to pet. Nancy was going. And Allen . . .

Allen was free. And although he had never been aware of her in anything but a brotherly way, she might, if she went home, be able to help him — even if all she could do was listen while he spoke of Nancy. She could look at him, at last, without having to remind herself that he belonged to another woman — and that woman Nancy. She could be with him. She could spend the lengthening spring days wandering with him on the farm as he worked, following him from task to task, sometimes helping, sometimes merely watching. She could see him, hear him. Allen . . .

"Well?" asked Nancy.

"Yes," Jendy said. "Yes, I'll go."

CHAPTER 2

She did not go at once. She stayed at the flat for a few days after Nancy's departure, putting away some of her things, finishing her work with the author and, lying in her bed at night, trying to imagine life at Tallahouse without Nancy.

It was not, she thought, going to be without its difficulties. Aunt Eddie was a powerful personality, and Jendy knew that she had not Nancy's easy way of managing her. Life alone at Tallahouse with seventy-three-year-old, overbearing, dictatorial Aunt Eddie. . . .

Aunt Eddie. Last of the Latimers of Tallahouse. Last of the long, long line.

Tallahouse had been the home of the Latimers since 1583. A large, beautiful Elizabethan building, it stood on a horseshoe curve of road that left the Devonshire village of Oxterley on its northern end and, winding around a low hill, rejoined it to the south.

The house had been little altered since its erection. A bathroom or two had been added, candles had given way to lamps, lamps to gas and gas to electricity, but for the most part, the owners of Tallahouse had left to their descendants the trouble and expense of installing contemporary amenities. It had been kept wind- and water-proof, but it contained few additions that could have added to the warmth or comfort of its tenants. Since the Latimers were not as a rule of a hospitable turn of mind, it did not disturb them to discover that friends, having come once to stay, did not come again.

Tallahouse's first owner had been a character even more picturesque than the house: Jendiss Talla, a dark-complexioned beauty from nobody ever discovered quite where, who appeared in England shortly after Drake's return from his voyages in 1580, followed him to Tavistock and declared her intention of remaining with him forever. History has no record of Drake's reaction to this proposal, but Mistress Talla departed from Tavistock and was next noticed in the village of Oxterley, twenty miles away. Here she took the fancy of Hugh Bertrand Latimer, a rich merchant who — it was claimed by subsequent generations of Latimers, despite a lamentable lack of proof — married her and built for her a beautiful house which he named after her. Here in due course Jendiss died, leaving a dozen dusky children whose descendants, in spite of repeated dilutions of Anglo-Saxon blood, obstinately retained something of the original Jendiss's Spice Island look.

Aunt Eddie — Miss Edwina Latimer — was the last of the direct line that began with Jendiss. She had been one of three children; her sister Jendiss had married late in life, borne Nancy and another Jendiss, and died shortly afterward. Her brother, Bertrand, died at about the same time, at the age of fifty. Nancy and Jendy had no recollection of him, but they knew that Aunt Eddie considered him guilty of monstrous and tragic selfishness in refusing to marry and beget a new generation of Latimers. She had found for him, she explained, several suitable women; he had rejected them all, betrayed his trust and allowed the long Talla line to die out.

After his death, Edwina had gone to a good deal of trouble to trace the Latimer nearest in kin. She at last discovered him living in Canada, and had offered to bequeath the house to him. After sending an English friend of his to look over it, he wrote to thank her, but firmly declined the offer.

There had been in every generation of Latimers a girl named Jendiss. Jendy did not count, since she was born Jendiss Marsh. Her mother had been, to Aunt Eddie's bitter regret, the last Jendiss Latimer of Tallahouse.

The day on which Jendy drove down to Devonshire was dull and rainy. It was about five o'clock when she reached Oxterley, but she did not take the direct route to Tallahouse through the village; she went, as she always did, the long way around the hill.

On the slopes of this, only four houses stood. She soon passed the first of these: Ravenscroft, an ugly, square-built, depressing-looking house surrounded by thick evergreen hedges. It had been occupied, ever since Jendy could remember, by a series of tenants, none of whom had stayed long enough or been interested enough in the place to improve the neglected and overgrown garden, which extended on one side to the borders of Farhills Farm.

Smoke was rising from the chimneys, indicating that the house was once more occupied, but Jendy noted the fact without interest, for the reason for her detour was coming into view: the first glimpses of Farhills itself.

In summer, nothing was to be seen of the farmhouse but its chimneys — but now, in spring, there were still enough bare branches between the evergreens to give a view of the lovely old building. Jenny brought the car to a halt, switched off the engine and sat looking at the view she remembered so well and loved so much.

She could see the garden, with the blue shadows of the hills creeping across it as dusk closed in. Lights glowed, one by one, in the farm buildings. The gray of the sky lightened to a delicate pink, deepened and then slowly faded. The hills darkened and the peace of the quiet countryside stole in upon her, bringing the sense of calm and freedom from care that invariably accompanied the sight of the house.

She sat on, looking at the lovely scene and trying to understand how Nancy could have resisted its spell. But Nancy, she realized, wanted other things. Color. There was color here, but it was subdued; every shade of green from tender new shoots to the near-black of the shadowed trees — but no crimson, no purple, no vivid, dramatic patches. Nancy wanted excitement, and there was none here; life flowed quietly, evenly, without the restless movement which she had come to mistake for living. She spoke of beauty, and beauty was here, but it changed only with the seasons. There was peace, but peace was something she felt should come only when passion ended.

Farhills — and Allen Harvey — were here. Nancy was far away.

A sense of waste gripped and held her. Something had been thrown away — something precious. . . .

Presently she drove on. The road curved, and she came to the neat little house named Gannets, and found herself accelerating in order to pass it as quickly as possible. Neither she nor Nancy had ever lingered when going past the house, for they had always been anxious to avoid the occupants — in the old days, dull old Colonel and Mrs. Druce and their far-from-dull daughter Anabel; today, Anabel's brother Milford.

Past Gannets for half a mile — and then before her was the four-hundred-year-old gateway of Tallahouse. Beyond was the long, neglected, weed-covered drive.

The car bumped over the uneven ground, and then Jendy drove under an archway of tall birches and stopped before the house which had been her home, and Nancy's, since the death of their parents more than twenty-five years ago.

She got out and stood looking up at the glint of the setting sun on the great hall window. From ground level almost to roof height, the three thousand small, square panes glowed blood-red. Above, the tall, graceful chimneys with their coupled shafts rose toward a sky that seemed to be an endless purple canopy.

She walked to the porch, pausing to look up at the heraldic stone panel above the door. In this light it looked almost terra cotta, and she thought that it had a sinister appearance, as though it knew that Nancy had rejected this house, this place. . . .

She heard the door opening. Dolly, sole maid in a house that required and had once held a dozen, stood before her, smiling in welcome. Jendy took the bony old hand in hers and greeted her affectionately and then went, as usual, straight upstairs to her room. Aunt Eddie never received her nieces until they had removed the stains of travel.

She had a bath, unpacked her things and then went down the broad staircase with its short, straight flights and wide landings. Her hands brushed, from childhood habit, the tall newel posts, and on the top of each she saw the carved effigies of the first Jendiss — one of the countless proofs the house held of the fact that it had been built for her, and built with love.

She opened the heavy door of the drawing room, went in and kissed the leathery cheek her aunt offered her.

"It's nice to be home, Aunt Eddie," she said.

"Ha," said Aunt Eddie, and Jendy translated the monosyllable correctly: her aunt was pleased to see her.

Miss Latimer was tall, stiff-backed, white-haired, with a beautifully boned face, the alert Talla nose and small, shrewd brown eyes that gazed suspiciously out at the world. Strangers found her manner a little intimidating at first, and more intimidating later on; few people cared to continue the acquaintance long enough to find out what lay beneath the uncompromising exterior.

When she was not issuing orders, Aunt Eddie was airing her opinions. She held strong views on almost everything, and saw no reason why people should not listen to them. She claimed to be interested in the opinions of others, but few people succeeded in voicing any in her presence.

She took an active interest in the affairs of the straggling little village of Oxterley, and had proved over and over again that it was no use trying to keep scandal or secrets from her. Her mind was as strong, as active and as tireless as her body, and she despised the modern tendency to warmth and comfort in the home.

"I'm glad you got here," she said, as Jendy sat down. Her voice was crisp and dry. "But I must say that in the circumstances, I expected to see you sooner."

"I had things to do. And Nancy didn't go until —"

"I never want to hear her name spoken again in this house," said Aunt Eddie. "Didn't go until when?"

"She stayed with me for three days."

"Oh, she did? When she left here, it looked as though she couldn't get back to Madrid fast enough. They say there's madness in every old family, and it certainly came out in her. What did you do for three days?"

"Tried to persuade her to stay, mostly."

"You were wasting your time."

"I know. But I couldn't bear to see her . . . I couldn't let her go without at least trying."

"Allen Harvey tried. I tried. We both —
Where are you going?"

Jendy was going to the cupboard in which
she and Nancy kept the sherry that Aunt
Eddie refused to touch. Under the unwinking
brown stare, she poured out a glass and
carried it to her chair.

"To keep up your strength?" inquired her
aunt acidly.

"To make me enjoy the half-hour before
dinner. What were you saying?"

"What does it matter? You were thinking
about your sherry."

"We were talking about Nancy."

"Which was a waste of time. She's gone,
and I dare say she won't come back. It's
throwing God's gifts in His face to refuse a
man like Allen Harvey, but it's done and
she's gone. And don't tell me there isn't
another man."

Jendy, who had raised the glass to her
lips, lowered it slowly and stared at her aunt,
too astounded to speak.

"W-what did you say?" she said at last.

"You heard quite well what I said. If you
didn't ask Nancy the question outright,
you're even more naïve than I've always
thought you. You're a nice girl, Jendy, and

you've got a nice mind, but you should give it some work to do sometimes. If there's a man like Allen Harvey handy, with plenty of money, a lovely home, a good job and a splendid character to offer a woman, why would she turn him down unless there was some man somewhere else she fancied? One of those Spaniards, I dare say, with tight trousers and flat hat and sidewhiskers."

"She loves Allen. She said she loved him, and I believe her."

"There you go again," snapped Aunt Eddie. "You've always been a girl who liked to dig a hole in the sand and bury your head in it when there were any hard facts to be faced. Nancy has gone to a man."

"Nancy has not."

"Well, we'll see, if we wait. And while we're waiting, ring that bell and I can order dinner."

Jendy rang the bell and spoke in a tone she kept deliberately casual.

"How is Allen?" she asked.

"He's a quiet man; you don't get to know all he's thinking," Aunt Eddie said, and there was regret in her voice. "He came up here before she left, and stood over her as though I was going to attack her. And all the time, watching her making her preparations for going away, I thought what a waste it all was. I thought, too, how time shows up our mistakes. Not that I hadn't realized for years that you had twice Nancy's intelligence and twice her stability, and in your way, just as much in the way of looks. But I — Is anything amusing you?"

"Yes. You." Jendy's smile widened. "You know perfectly well that Nancy makes me look . . . Well, let's say it's the old comparison between the sun and the moon."

"You being the moon?"

"Yes. I know quite well what people feel about Nancy, because I feel the same myself."

"So did I. But I don't any more. It's not only because she's killed my hope of seeing her settled at Farhills, settled near me and perhaps having a troupe of children I could enjoy while I lived. It's that — You're surely not going to have *another* drink?"

"Yes," said Jendy from the cupboard. "I am. Why can't you be like other old ladies, and take a drink of some sort now and then?"

"Because, unlike other old ladies, I'm hale and vigorous enough without it. And — *Now* what's amusing you?"

"Us."

"And what is so amusing about us?"

"This scene." Jendy looked around the oak-paneled room, with its elaborate ceiling molded in intricte geometrical patterns. Her eyes rested on the carved stone figures above the fireplace, which showed Jendiss Talla in the Garden of Eden with an Adam who bore a marked resemblance to her husband. "If you put it all on paper," she said, "you could make it sound almost cozy. Scene One: drawing room of historic old house, soft lights, curtains drawn against the cold spring evening, charming old lady in high-backed chair, charming young niece seated opposite, clock chiming seven-thirty, faithful old maid coming in to prepare the table for dinner. On paper."

"And off paper?"

"Well, hardly cozy," pointed out Jendy. "The grate's meant to burn sizable tree trunks, and all it's got in it are a few smoldering logs. The charming old lady's wearing a thick tweed skirt, two thick woolen sweaters —"

"Cardigans."

"Cardigans, and a pair of wool-lined bootees. The charming niece is in warm trousers and footwear of —"

"Extraordinary footwear, if you'll permit

me to say so."

"— of the type known as après-ski. The faithful old maid will fetch a card table from a corner, open it and lay it for dinner. After dinner, she'll clear it and niece will fetch aunt's patience cards and then there'll be silence until it's time to go to bed."

"Is that the end?"

"Yes. Curtain."

"I suppose it's uncomfortable in some ways," acknowledged Aunt Eddie, "but whenever the question of heating the place arises, all you have to do is think of the cost — and you leave things as they are. Have you any idea what it costs to keep a house like this merely standing up and in good condition?"

"Heaps, I suppose."

"Well, we did it. And when I'm dead, we won't do it any more. Nancy won't want it and neither will you — unless you marry a rich man."

She paused, her eyes absently following Dolly's movements as she prepared the table. When she went out, she looked at Jendy.

"Speaking of marriage," she said, "is there any special young man? You tell me nothing in your letters."

"No special man," said Jendy.

"Has anybody proposed to you?"

"Yes."

"And you said?"

"No."

"Why? Are you sure you're not leaving it too long? You're going on for twenty-five, and the older a woman gets, the more choosey she becomes. If that meant she'd choose better as time went on, one would encourage it, but unfortunately it's as easy to be a fool at thirty as at twenty. Like Nancy. If she'd married Allen when he first asked her, when she was eighteen, she would have been better off now. What happened to that nice young man who used to drive you down here before you had your car?"

"He married someone else."

"They do," said Aunt Eddie. "You close your eyes for a moment to consider their eligibility, and when you open them, they've vanished. That's how it is I never married, and that's why I like to see a girl take a good man while she can get him. That's how it was your mother let several fine fellows get away, and ended up with a run-of-the-mill man like your father."

"Judging by their letters, they were very happy."

"Is there any reason why she shouldn't

have been equally happy with a man who could provide for her properly? I warned her that he'd never have a penny, and he never did. Now draw up your chair and eat your soup."

"I thought," said Jendy, over the soup, "that you'd got television."

"I had it."

"And then?"

"I sent it away again. I wasn't going to sit night after night with my hands folded, staring into a little square box. If I enjoyed it, I thought it was a waste of time. If I didn't, I thought it was a waste of even more time. So I sent it away. How long are you going to be at home this time?"

Jendy hesitated. This evening, she knew, was a sample of all the other evenings. She had long ago decided that life offered more than this chilly room and Aunt Eddie's monologues. But tonight she was seeing Tallahouse with eyes that seemed to have grown clearer. Aunt Eddie's manner, astringent though it might be, had something stimulating in it. For the first time in her life, she felt something like pride at being the daughter of Jendiss Latimer of Talla-house, and regret that there would be no more Jendiss Latimers to come.

41

"I'll stay as long as you want me," she said.

There was a pause. Aunt Eddie broke her bread into several small pieces and arranged them absently around her plate.

"I might want you," she said at last, "for quite a long time. I shall tell you frankly that Nancy has left me feeling shaken. As I told you, I've revised my estimate of her."

"If she wanted to go back to Spain, she had a right to go. It's her life, and she has a right to lead it in her own way."

"And that's where you're wrong. She has no right," said Aunt Eddie, "to lead it in a way that hurts other people. Allen was never very sure of her — but I think that when she came back four months ago, he allowed himself to believe that it would be all right. The fact that she'd had time to think it over, had thought it over and had come back to him must have made him feel, at last, that she was going to settle. If it hadn't been for that brother of his, she never would have got unsettled in the first place."

"Brother? You mean Roderick?"

"As Allen only has one brother, naturally I mean Roderick. If he hadn't come back from his wanderings and filled Nancy's head with nonsense, she would never have left

42

Tallahouse. It was all very well for him to decide that England was a dull old place and that everybody should go and live in Spain, but it's a pity he came back here and persuaded Nancy to think the same."

"You really think that if it hadn't been for Roderick, she —"

"— would have stayed here perfectly contentedly until she married Allen and went to live at Farhills. And now, if you please, he's going to settle down there himself."

"*Roderick* is?"

"I wish you'd keep your mind on what people are saying. We are still talking about Roderick. Didn't Nancy tell you that he was building a house on the Farhills land?"

"No."

"Perhaps she had more important things on her mind. He's putting up a house on the slope that overlooks Ravenscroft. He came down here just after Nancy left, and he brought a sheaf of plans and an architect and a builder and a gang of workmen, and they all set to work at once. If Allen had asked my advice, I would have told him that I thought the idea a bad one. A house with a studio, if you please. Going to paint seriously, he said. 'Seriously?' I said. 'You've never done anything serious in your whole life.' "

"You saw him?"

"He came here to see me. I can't say I was cordial. I never liked him and I never will. I asked him what would have happened to the farm if Allen, like himself, had shed all his responsibilities when his parents died, and skipped off to do his daubing on the Continent? He had nothing to answer to that."

Jendy was assembling her recollections of Roderick Harvey. A year younger than his brother, he had, like Allen, been born and brought up at Farhills. But Allen had rarely left the farm, while Roderick, from boyhood, had seldom been at home. He had spent most of his school holidays and subsequent Oxford vacations with friends, at first in England and then abroad. Jendy had gone to live in London, and their visits home had rarely coincided. She recalled, now, his length and leanness, his brown face and dark, unreadable eyes. She also recalled her faint dislike of him; he had been in every way the reverse of Allen, and Allen had been her hero, her ideal of what a man should be. Allen was predictable, dependable and unfailingly kind. Roderick's lazy, relaxed manner was deceptive; beneath it, she knew from experience, was alertness and a disconcerting

44

ability to read her mind. Allen was approachable; a homely, familiar figure. Roderick was detached and aloof; a man impossible to gauge.

"And after Roderick arrived with his entourage," she heard her aunt saying, "who d'you think put in an appearance?"

"Some of his foreign friends?"

"No. You'll never guess. Anabel."

Jendy stared at her, unwilling to believe the bad news.

"Anabel?" she echoed in a tone of dismay.

"Anabel Druce. I knew you'd be delighted. She only missed Nancy by a day or so."

"You don't mean she's going to stay here?"

"If you want my opinion, she's going to stay here just as long as Roderick Harvey does."

"But —"

"If you're going to say she's married, you'll be wrong. She's free."

"*Another* divorce?"

"Yes. That'll make the third." Aunt Eddie counted on her fingers. "The first was when she was twenty, when she got rid of her Household Cavalry, or whoever he was. Then there was the American one; he got rid of her when she was about twenty-three or four. This time, she's cast off a foreign title — Spanish, if I'm not mistaken. You can't say she's wasted her time; she's exactly the same age as Nancy, isn't she?"

"Yes."

"Well, you can take it from me that husband number four is going to be Roderick Harvey. She's been after him since she was in her teens. Every time she came home, she made a dead set for him. Allen was never her type; she was content to leave Allen to Nancy — but if Nancy had ever looked at Roderick, there would have been blood spilled. And now Roderick's here for good, and she's free and she might succeed in cornering him. On the other hand, he's a slippery customer, and I dare say he's used to dealing with women like her. I hope she gets him. He deserves it."

"Where's she staying?"

"Where else but at Gannets?"

"At *Gannets?*" Jendy's voice rose with surprise. "But Milford —"

"Milford should have known he couldn't trust her. I told him so at the time. He bought her share of the house at an absurdly high figure when the old people died, on the express condition that she'd keep away and let him occupy it alone. But now she's back, and she's brought her nasty little daughter with her. You've never seen her, have you?"

"No. And I don't think I've seen Anabel more than twice since her parents died."

"No great hardship for you. Though you weren't her chief enemy. It was Nancy she was always so jealous of."

"She loathed us both. And we loathed her. How's Milford standing up to it?"

"Badly. How long is it since you saw him?"

"About two years."

"He's looking older since Anabel came back. He never looked forty before. He's still got that married couple looking after him, but with Anabel and Beulah — Beulah's the daughter — making hay of the house, he's frightened they'll give notice. He can't sleep for worrying. He'd just got the house as he wanted it: all his little knickknacks, his Siamese cats and his little Greek statues in the garden."

"I suppose he still does his own cooking?"

"He still makes his own little messes. French food cooked in Swedish dishes and served up on Italian pottery. I always refuse now, when he asks me to dine with him; you can't taste the food for the sauce. When I told him you were coming back, he got

47

quite excited."

"What's Anabel's name now?"

"What does it matter? Nobody can keep pace. Everybody down here still calls her Druce. She won't come here, of course; she knows what I think of her. She'll spend all her time at Farhills, stalking Roderick Harvey, and it'll be hard on Allen, for he never could bear her. Which reminds me: Allen wants to see you."

Jendy's heart contracted.

"He wants . . ."

"You'd better go down to Farhills tomorrow. He wants to talk to you. And I'd like you to talk to him; you might be able to make things easier. You can at least listen while he talks about Nancy."

Jendy went down the following evening. She took the car, for it was growing dark; she had chosen a time when she knew that Allen would be finishing his work and making his way to the house for a drink, a bath, a change — and dinner.

She left the car in the yard and walked slowly through the wide white gate leading to the stackyard. Thick clouds were spreading across the sky, darkening the last rays of the sun. She had a feeling that a door had closed behind her, leaving her alone in a place that suddenly seemed strangely unfamiliar.

She glanced toward the house and saw lights beginning to spring up in the windows, and wondered whether Allen was already inside — and then she heard his footsteps crossing the yard and coming toward the gate.

She turned and watched him as he came toward her, counting, as she waited, the time that had passed since she had done more than stop for a brief greeting at the beginning or the end of her visits to Tallahouse. How many years . . . ? And during those years, she had tried to forget him — but as she looked at him now, she knew that she had remembered every detail of his face with faithful clarity.

He was six feet in height, but so broad that he was not generally taken for a tall man. He was brown-haired, gray-eyed, slow-moving, dressed in a worn tweed jacket and leather gaiters. He was bareheaded; he had been walking slowly, with bent head, engrossed in his own thoughts, and then he caught sight of Jendy and halted, staring at her for some moments as though he could not believe his eyes.

Then he came toward her with long, eager

strides, his face alight with welcome. They met without speaking; Jendy could not find anything to say, and he was absorbed in noting changes in her. She had grown more slender, he thought — or taller — and certainly lovelier. But though lovely, she was fair and not dark; though tall, not tall enough. Her voice, when she spoke, was musical, but it was not husky with laughter, not deep with excitement or tremulous with feeling. . . . She was Nancy's sister, lovely of face and figure. But she was not Nancy.

"Well, Jendy," he said at last. "You're really here? For how long?"

"As long as Aunt Eddie wants me."

Her hands were in his, and she drew them gently away.

"Were you going inside?" she asked.

"No. I was going along to one of the cottages to pay a fellow some money I owe him. Look — will you go up to the house? Pour yourself out a drink, and I'll be up before you have time to finish it."

She walked to the house and Dan, the old man who acted as cook and housekeeper, led her to the drawing room, switched on a light and left her alone.

She stood in the middle of the room and looked about her and tried not to think of

Nancy. She had pictured her with Allen in this house, in this beautiful, quiet, low-beamed room. Nancy and Allen together at the end of each busy day.

Suddenly the confusion, the fears, the stresses of the past days overwhelmed her. She sat on the old-fashioned sofa, put her head down on the arm and wept. She wept openly, unrestrainedly, making no attempt to control her grief, her regrets for Nancy, her pity for the man Nancy had left. Weeping, she felt some of the tension within her ease.

After a time, she groped for a spare handkerchief. With her head still on the sofa arm, she felt in one coat pocket and then another.

And then a hand — a man's hand — put a folded one into her searching fingers.

She thought that it was Allen — and then she saw that it was not his square, strong hand. These fingers were long, brown, nervous — the fingers of an artist.

She looked up to find Roderick Harvey standing beside her.

"I've got another one if you need it," he said.

She shook her head, angry and ashamed at having been surprised by someone with eyes that saw as much as this man's. But he was showing nothing save a grave politeness, and she accepted the handkerchief, unfolded it and dried her tears. Then she spoke shakily.

"I'm sorry," she said. "I just . . . I just felt awful, that's all. Sitting in here, it all seemed so . . . pointless and so . . . so idiotic and . . ."

He said nothing. He looked taller and leaner than she remembered, and there was something in his air — something detached and, she thought, unsympathetic — that brought the color to her cheeks and made her regret more than ever her display of emotion. She blew her nose angrily and met his gaze.

"You think," he said, "that Nancy has been foolish?"

Tears sprang once more to her eyes, and she fought them back.

"I think," she said tremulously, "that she doesn't really know what she's doing."

"At twenty-seven?"

His tone was one of polite inquiry, but she felt anger flooding her. And then through the uncurtained window she saw Allen's torch wavering in the darkness, and knew that Roderick had seen it too.

"Here's Allen," he said.

Panic seized her. She searched agonizedly for lipstick, for powder, for anything that would repair the ravages to her face. She had no time to think of Roderick, but through her feverish preparations, she was aware that his eyes were on her, knew that he was taking note of her agitation and drawing his own conclusions.

"I hope you're going to stay down here for some time," he said.

She looked at him, in her eyes something that was almost an appeal.

"Do you think I . . . do you think I should? I mean . . ."

"Allen will be very glad to have you here," he said. "I hope you won't go away."

She sat staring straight before her, and he followed her thoughts without difficulty. Allen was alone, and perhaps she could help him. Nancy had gone. Nancy . . . Nancy had had her chance — and had thrown it away.

She met Roderick Harvey's eyes, and she was too deep in dreams of her own to realize how much she gave away.

"You really think I could help him?" she asked.

His thick, winged eyebrows went up, but

his tone was quiet and even.

"Yes, I do," he said. "Will you stay?"

She hesitated. Allen's step sounded outside.

"Yes, I'll stay," she said.

CHAPTER 3

The next morning, Jendy breakfasted alone and then went upstairs to pay her morning visit to Aunt Eddie who, sitting bolt upright in bed in a fireless bedroom, was drinking strong tea and eating well-buttered toast.

"You slept well?" she asked, as Jendy entered the room.

"Beautifully, thank you." Jendy bent and kissed her. "And you?"

"I always sleep well. What are your plans for the day?"

"I thought I might do your shopping for you, or help Dolly."

"I always walk down to the village and give my own orders, and Dolly prefers to work alone. If you want to do something really useful," said Aunt Eddie, "you'll go down to Farhills, as you used to do in the old days. It'll cheer Allen up."

"He'll probably be busy."

"When did that ever keep you or Nancy away? He won't stop working in order to chat to you, but he'll be pleased to know you're there. You can bring a few eggs back with you."

Jendy needed no urging. She put on her strongest shoes, looked at the threatening sky, put a mackintosh around her shoulders and let herself out of the house.

As she walked past Gannets, she saw, to her relief, no sign of Anabel. Hurrying by, she reached the white gates of Farhills, walked into the yard and stood looking about her.

Yesterday, the farm had looked strange; she had found it almost unfriendly — but then she had been depressed, half-longing, half-dreading to meet Allen. Now, in the morning light, she saw all around her the buildings, the objects she had known since her childhood, and she remembered with gratitude the years of happiness that this place had given her — and given Nancy.

She looked over to the long line of cowsheds, built by Allen's father, who had pointed out that he provided far more comfort for his cows than Aunt Eddie enjoyed at Tallahouse. She wandered toward them, remembering half-forgotten names: Hebe, Phoebe, Ondine — and Jessamine, who had arrived at the farm on a snowy Easter Day, and had been installed with Jendy's help into her new home.

She went on slowly past the granary, past the stone-floored dairy with its humming milk-cooling plant and din of clashing bottles, and stopped to greet the woman working inside. She had been dairywoman as long as Jendy could remember: worn and aged and wrinkled, but strong and tireless.

There was no sign of Allen. She walked along the path that led to the orchard and leaned against the fence, gazing at the first sign of blossom on the trees, pink and white on the dark, wet branches. Calves, eyeing her from a distance, came slowly nearer until at last their soft mouths nuzzled her palms. At the far end of the orchard she saw the great bull, Julius, bred by Allen, and famous throughout the countryside. Jendy called to him, and he gave her a look of watchful contempt before rubbing his head against a tree trunk.

The April sun came out and warmed her face. The air held a hundred familiar sounds; sounds that brought memories of half-forgotten incidents, half-forgotten people, all of them connected with the farm. Tallahouse had been her home, but this place had been her playground. Hers — and Nancy's.

And then above the song of the birds and the creaking of cart wheels, she heard her name called, and turned to see Allen coming toward her, striding down the wooded lane that led from the house to the farm.

"How long have you been here?" he asked, as he came.

"Not long. I've been standing here remembering things."

"Being chased by a bull less chivalrous than Julius, for example?"

"I'd forgotten that. What was his name?"

"His full name was Farhills Emperor. I never saw a girl run so fast."

She laughed.

"Can I stay for a while?"

"You can stay all day." His voice was warm, and she colored with pleasure. "You can come every day and all day and follow me around as you used to do in the old days, watching me work."

"You weren't always working."

"True. But that was when I was merely a farmer's son. Once I had to run the whole show, leisure vanished. Have you decided how long you're going to stay down here?"

"Quite a long time, I think."

"Good. With Nancy gone, Aunt Eddie'll need you."

The words were said easily, almost casually, and Jendy felt a surge of relief. They were, then, to talk of Nancy freely and naturally, as she longed to do. Last night, she had waited for him to speak of her — and he had not done so.

Her heart almost light, she walked with him toward the house.

"I was inside, and I saw you from a window and came out to fetch you. I'm looking up some milk records; you can come and help me."

"Aunt Eddie told me that Anabel Druce is home," she said on the way to the house.

"It's not her home — it's Milford's, and she should never have come back," he said. "They never got on, and she promised to leave him in peace. She was too clever to let him know she was coming. She just arrived — with Beulah. Milford came down here to tell me about it, and cried — really cried. He'd just cooked himself one of his little dinners and was sitting down to enjoy it, when he heard the car, Anabel's car. And there they were, with luggage. He told me that he knows quite well she's after something; at the moment, he's not sure what it is, and I didn't enlighten him, but you'd better know now as later that it's Roderick."

"So Aunt Eddie said. How did Anabel know he was here?"

"She's always kept him in view. They met again in Spain — I suppose you know she was married to a Spaniard?"

"Yes. If she wanted Roderick so much, why —"

"— did she go off and marry other men? Hope flickers, hope dies. Roderick's not easy to pin down. She got to know that he'd come home and was building his own house — and here she is. Hope revives. She's been here every day since she came back — she and Beulah. Not an attractive child."

"What's she like?"

Allen ushered her into his study and gave his slow smile.

"Wait and see. I always like people to form their own opinions."

"Has Anabel changed?"

"She hasn't come near enough for me to decide. She spends all her time up at the site with Roderick."

"Without coming to speak to you?"

"Why should she waste time doing that? She was always single-minded; in that re-

60

spect, at any rate, she doesn't seem to have changed. I don't suppose she'll waste much time on you, either."

"When does Roderick expect the house to be finished?"

"End of the summer, he hopes. End of the year, I think. He wants to get the studio finished first."

"He still paints?"

"Very seriously — and very well." He looked up in surprise from the papers he had taken from his desk. "Surely you've seen some of his work?"

"Only the things hanging in this house, and a picture he gave Nancy in Spain."

"I like his things. So do a lot of people who know more about painting than I do." He placed a chair at the desk for Jendy. "Odd life, isn't it? I hoped that Nancy would live here one day — but I was sure that Roderick never would. I felt it in my bones. Unreliable bones, because she's gone and he's here to stay."

"Will he really settle? He always seemed to me —"

"— the unsettled type? You mustn't let his manner mislead you. You mustn't let Aunt Eddie mislead you, either. She's always regarded him as the farm's black sheep."

"Why? Was it because he spent so much time abroad?" she asked.

"I suppose you could put it that way. It was because he spent so little time here. She thought he ought to have been as keen on running the farm as I was. Well, he wasn't. He didn't want to farm, and I did. But Aunt Eddie was very fond of my father, and she thought that Roderick disappointed him."

"And did he?"

"Disappoint him? No. He was quite content to see each of us go our own way. My father managed the farm on his own, and so can I. But I didn't imagine that Roderick would ever come back and make his home here. It's the best thing that's happened to me since . . . well, since Nancy came back from Spain and I thought she'd got the bug out of her system."

Jendy was at the window, looking at the rising ground on which the house was being built. Allen came to stand beside her.

"We chose the site together," he said. "I'll see the chimneys of the house, but no more. He's kept those trees as a screen, so that he won't overlook me. At the moment, he's having to use the farm entrance, but he's planning to buy a piece of ground from the owners of Ravenscroft, and then he'll make a road through it and be entirely self-contained."

"Will they sell?"

"I don't see why they shouldn't. The place has always had too much ground for the tenants to manage. It's a hell of a wilderness now. I should think they'd be glad to let Roderick buy a chunk of it."

The door opened, and they turned to see Roderick in the doorway.

"We were just talking about your house," Allen told him.

"You shouldn't be talking about anything," Roderick said. "There's a fellow over in the cowsheds waiting for you to produce some figures. Milk yields or butterfat percentages, whichever."

"It's Jendy's fault. Take her away."

"That's what I was going to do." Roderick spoke with calm assurance. "She's coming up to see how my house is getting on."

Jendy went unwillingly. She had been happy and absorbed in Allen's company, but there was something about Roderick that made her feel uncomfortable. She tried to analyze the reason for this, and came to the conclusion that it sprang from her distrust of his manner, which was at once casual and faintly provocative. She had the impression that he was watching her — and watching her with amusement.

She would have liked to ask him what had become of Anabel, but she said nothing. Walking up the steep path to the building site, however, she admitted to herself that he was well worth Anabel's attention. Tall and dark and interesting-looking, she told herself, if you liked them that way — and of course Anabel did. Not as broad as Allen; not as good-looking. Not as easy to talk to — but undoubtedly a man of the kind the Anabels always seemed to seek out. Elusive. Deep. Yes, that was it: deep. He said something in a perfectly ordinary tone of voice, but when you chanced to look up suddenly, you saw a calculating look in his eye. Calculating? Not exactly. More like assessing. Not a man she herself could ever get on with — though some people would no doubt call him outstandingly attractive.

He put out a hand, took one of hers and helped her up the slope. There were several men at work, and Roderick introduced each of them to Jendy.

"Good fellows all," he told her, "and — except for the tea breaks — good workers. You'd better see the view first. That, after all, was what brought me back to Farhills.

Stand here and imagine you're on my balcony — glassed-in, with folding doors you can open in warm weather."

Jendy, gazing out over the beautiful scene, drew a deep breath.

"It's . . . it's lovely. I'm glad you're not going to cut down the trees."

"Only enough to give me a so-called vista. I didn't want to overlook Farhills and I didn't want to spoil the hillside by letting the house show too much. See that slope? Terraced gardens — one day. The only thing I need is a bit more land on the other side."

"The side that joins the Ravenscroft grounds?"

"Yes. I'm trying to locate the owner. I want to make an offer for that wasted bit of garden nobody's ever wanted. Come along and I'll show you."

He led her around the shoulder of the hill, and she saw beyond them, through the trees, the upper windows of Ravenscroft.

"The house isn't too near," said Roderick, "but if I could get a bit of the land, I'd make a nice tree-lined drive out on to the road."

"Who owns the house?" Jendy asked.

"I haven't found out yet. It's always been in the hands of the Tavistock agents, and it's been let furnished — if you can call it furniture — ever since I can remember. Nobody's done anything to the place for years. It looks a shambles. Perhaps that's why it attracts such odd tenants."

"Odd?"

"Allen says they've all been peculiar in some way or another. I can't remember them all, because I've been away so much, but I do remember the Swedish couple who used to keep Great Danes."

"When I was about ten," Jendy recalled, "there was a Greek family living there. Nancy and I used to come down to Farhills and walk up to this boundary and listen to them singing wailing songs."

"There was an old poet who was as mad as a hatter — and there was a woman who painted. She was before your time; I was only about eight or nine myself, but I can still remember what she used to dress in. Blue smock and red trousers. I used to peer through a hole in the hedge and watch her painting. Perhaps she sparked off in my little mind a desire to paint too. I got to know her a little — she used to give me lettuce sandwiches. Said she came from Brazil."

"Where's your garden going to be?" Jendy asked.

"Lawn and rose garden? There's not much

flat ground — just that patch over there."

"Quite a big patch."

"I've got a man coming to clear it — and I don't envy him the job. Come down this way — and mind how you go; it's pretty steep."

They walked down to the farmhouse, and he put a casual question.

"How do you find Allen?"

"I think he's . . . I think he's taken it wonderfully."

"Does he talk about Nancy?"

"Yes. Do you" — she looked up at him — "do you think he'll write to her?"

"Why don't you ask him?"

She did not reply. She was seeing for the first time certain details of his features that resembled Allen's. She had thought of the two as entirely different types, but she saw now that their eyes were alike — not in color, for Allen's were lighter and clearer — but alike in shape and setting: deep, beneath winged eyebrows. Their mouths were also alike, but she had always loved Allen's mouth for what she had thought of as its defenselessness. There was nothing about Roderick's that suggested anything but firmness and confidence.

He raised his eyebrows sardonically at her

scrutiny, but she was becoming used to his manner.

"Won't you find it dull down here?" she asked.

"I shall be working: painting. When I'm working, I'm never dull."

"You've been abroad so much, won't you miss the sun?"

"If I do, I'll pay it a visit. Is Nancy glad to be back in the sun?"

"I've only had one letter so far."

"Is she in the same place in Madrid?"

"She isn't in Madrid. She left almost as soon as she arrived, and went down to stay with some friends in Seville."

"Seville?"

There was something in his tone that told her he was surprised — and something more. But the something more was hidden almost instantly behind the casualness of his next words, and she could as usual read nothing in his glance.

"Spanish friends?" he inquired. "I know a good many of her friends out there."

She went through the pockets of her coat and brought out the letter.

"They're called" — she searched for and found the name — "Navarrete."

"Navarrete?"

He gave the word its four syllables, with the slight roll of the two r's in the middle, and the pictures that had formed in Jendy's mind as she read the letter, of people familiar and recognizable, vanished; in their place were Spaniards of the kind that tourists did not meet; hidden; apart. And in his voice, too, had been once more the uneasy surprise that he had shown for an instant at the mention of Seville.

"Do you know them?" she asked him.

"Very well, indeed."

"Are they nice?"

"They've got a palace in Madrid and a palace in Seville and unlimited money and an army of servants and a tinge of royal blood."

"I see. Are they nice?"

"What do you mean by nice?" He asked the question soberly, as though he really wanted to know. "Moral? Well-mannered? Well-meaning?"

She felt herself growing angry, but she persisted.

"If you hear that your sister's staying with some people, you like to hear what they're like," she pointed out. "Nancy never mentioned them to me."

"Never mentioned the Navarretes?"

There was again surprise, again something more in his tone.

"She certainly didn't tell me she was going to stay with them."

"Her business is her business. But it's quite a feat to be able to talk of Madrid or Seville for long without mentioning the Navarretes. They're the center, the core, the axis of all the foreigners in the place. That is, all the interesting foreigners. Nancy has known them for over a year."

"How do you know?"

"I introduced Carlos Navarrete to her. Carlos is the brother. There's a sister — married."

"Parents?"

"Elsewhere. So is the sister's husband."

"How old are they?"

"Carlos is about my age — thirty-three. Milagros must be twenty-eight."

"Milagros . . . doesn't that mean miracle?"

"It does."

His information had been given freely, almost carelessly, but she was certain that he knew a great deal more, and had no intention of disclosing it. Her anger mounted and showed in her cheeks, and he watched her with a kind of silent intentness, as he had done when he came upon her crying.

"If you know anything about these Spanish friends of yours that would make Allen uneasy," she said, "I'd rather you didn't tell him that Nancy's staying with them."

She saw him frown.

"I don't follow the reasoning," he said.

"Don't try to. All I'm asking you is not to fill Allen's mind with vague suspicions, as you've just filled mine. If you've got anything against them, why don't you say so? As soon as I mentioned their name, you shut up like a clam. I hate people who make mysteries when there's no need —"

"You're getting mixed up, aren't you?" he asked coldly. "We were talking about Nancy, not about me."

"I asked you if they were nice people and —"

"— and I forgot to mention that Carlos is far from nice. But Nancy obviously doesn't think so, because she saw a good deal of him when she was in Madrid, and I dare say she's seeing even more of him down in Seville. And the fact that he's not what you call nice needn't surprise you, because Nancy's just given a spectacular demonstration of the fact that she's no judge of a man."

71

"You've no right to —"

"If she'd rather go after Carlos Navarette than stay with Allen, it's her business and there's nothing you can do about it. She's twenty-seven; I reminded you of the fact last night. She's grown up; adult — in years — and she can do as she likes, even if it's what you don't like."

"You know nothing whatsoever about —"

"How can anybody be as old as you, as intelligent as you — and as naïve as you appear to be? Carlos and his sister are both very not-nice, and Nancy knows it and has just spent four months or so weighing them against Allen and deciding that she prefers what they've got — whatever it is. She had to tell you she was going to Seville, because she wants to get letters from you. Otherwise it's my guess she wouldn't have said a word about the Navarretes."

"I'd be very glad if you'd —"

"You'd better not mention them to your aunt, because she's got a gift for sizing up people she doesn't know. Me, for instance. And if you do mention them, you'd better not tell her that it was I who introduced them to Nancy; she's got enough against me without adding that. And now tell me, if you can, why you're so bent on prolonging

Allen's agony by keeping from him anything that could make him think less tenderly of Nancy?"

He stopped, awaiting her reply, but she was unable to speak. She was breathing with difficulty, and through her fury she knew dimly that she had never in her life had the smallest desire to strike anybody — until now. And now, she realized, she had two alternatives: to hit Roderick Harvey, very hard — or leave him at once.

She turned and left him. The incident had begun and ended so swiftly that rage and bewilderment were equally present in her mind. She went blindly toward the gates of the farm, and not until it was too late to avoid him did she encounter Allen.

There was no time to dissemble. He looked at her flushed, angry face, and a slow smile overspread his own.

"Well, well, well," he said. "So soon? Didn't I warn you about Roderick's misleading manner?"

With an effort, she managed to speak calmly.

"He's . . . provocative, to say the least," she said.

"It's a natural gift, and he's been polishing it for years. Shall I tell him to stop teasing you?"

"I'll tell him myself."

That, and other things, she resolved. She wasn't going to let Roderick Harvey make her lose her temper again. And she wasn't going to listen to him maligning Nancy's friends.

Nancy's? He had said that he had known them first. If he knew them, if the things he had hinted about them were true. . . .

"You're not going home so early?" she heard Allen asking. "There's lunch and to spare, if you'd stay."

"No, I won't stay, thanks." She had, suddenly, a strong desire to get away from the farm, to be alone, to think about the Navarretes — and about Nancy.

Allen walked to the gate with her.

"Come back this afternoon," he said. "And in the meantime, I'll carve Roderick up with the cold lamb."

"I'll manage Roderick."

"You won't," he prophesied. "Nobody's ever been able to do it. The best thing —"

He stopped. They had reached the gate, and blocking it they saw a small, mud-streaked black car to which was attached a trim and well-kept little caravan. The car was being driven by a young man, and beside him sat a girl of about twenty.

"This won't take long." Allen's voice was firm. "They come in droves, from now until the autumn, asking for parking space. What makes them think that a farm's a camping site?"

The driver of the car had got out and was approaching. He was not more than twenty-two or three. He was wearing blue jeans, a sky-blue sweater and a jaunty, scarlet woolen cap, on which was a fat white pompon. He stopped before Allen and Jendy, deferentially lifted the pompon two inches, and dropped it again.

" 'Morning," he said. His voice was light and cheerful, with unmistakably Cockney undertones. His hair was dark, his eyes brown, but what struck Jendy most was his serene, unruffled air, which seemed to indicate that he found the world both agreeable and accommodating.

"You wouldn't be Mr. Roderick Harvey?" he asked Allen, and answered the question himself. "No; you don't answer the description. You must be the other one. Your brother around, by any chance? He's got a job for me — so they told me in the village."

"He's up at the building site," Allen said.

"Well, that's where I'm bound. Booth's

the name. Wally Booth. Just call me Wally. I've come to do the clearing. Mind if I drive the caravan inside?"

"Yes, I do," said Allen. "The fact is —"

"I thought that as I'd be working here," Wally went on, "you'd let me shove the thing in one of your fields. That way, I could keep an eye on Greta. Greta's the girl friend. Hey — Greta."

The girl stepped out of the car. She was yellow-haired, distractingly pretty, and in an advanced stage of pregnancy.

"See what I mean?" asked Wally. "We had a look around the camping sites, but they're all on the other side of the village, and they don't come up to this place for scenery, if you foller me. How about it?"

There was a moment's hesitation, and then Allen pointed down the road.

"If you'll go along to the other gate and drive in," he said, "I'll show you where to park."

Wally, with a grin that said more than a whole sentence of thanks, raised the pompon once more and went back to the car.

"You stay here, Greta," he instructed the girl. "We don't want you bumping over fields. Swedish," he informed Jendy and Allen. "She's beautiful, isn't she?"

76

"Yes, she is," said Allen.

"And she's mine, that's what I can't get over," said Wally in wonder. "Mine, all mine, as the song —"

The rest of the sentence was lost in the sound of the engine. He drove slowly down the road, and Allen walked beside the car. Left with Jendy, the girl gave a warm, friendly smile.

"You live here?" she asked, in slow, careful English.

"No. I live about a mile away."

"In that big old house?"

The description could not be applied to Gannets or to Ravenscroft. Jendy nodded.

"We went to look at it," Greta told her. "Wally likes houses — old houses. We drove up to it and an old lady — your grand-mother?"

"My aunt."

"So old? She came out and told us to go away. She was angry. She thought perhaps that we were going to ask her if we could put the caravan there. You have to live with her?"

"No. I'm just staying for a time, but I was brought up in the house."

"By the old aunt?"

"Yes. She's rather intimidating, but —"

"In-tim-i-dating. That means to frighten?" Greta smiled. "Nobody can frighten Wally. He is un-frighten-able."

"So I should imagine. Do you like living in a caravan?"

"Yes, and then no. If Wally is with me, then of course I like it. He says that when we are married, we shall have a house."

"When you're —"

Jendy stopped abruptly, annoyed at having been taken off her guard. Roderick Harvey had called her naïve, and perhaps this proved it. She had only to glance at the girl's ringless hand to grasp the situation, even if Wally's reference to her as the girl friend had not already made the matter clear. It was disconcerting to find the other girl's gaze resting on her with an amused, quizzical glance.

"You are shocked?"

"No. I'm not shocked. I was just surprised, that's all."

"We are going to be married — one day. We —"

There was a loud hail, and they turned to see Wally coming toward them. Greta watched him as he drew near, on her face an expression at once indulgent and maternal.

"He is crazy," she said, "but he is good."

"All fixed," said Wally, joining them.

"Drinking water handy, free milk, nice view, and only four hundred yards to walk to work every morning." He took Greta's hand. "Come on. Come and cook my dinner."

"She lives at that house we saw," Greta told him. "The angry old lady is her aunt."

"You don't say?" Wally turned to Jendy, sympathy in his tone. "Bet she leads you a life."

"She's really very nice," said Jendy.

"She's really very nasty," said Wally. "She ought to be hung upside down three times a day to let the gall out of her."

"She lives alone in that big house when you go away?" Greta asked.

"She has a maid."

"A young one?"

"No. Old."

"Only one old servant for all that house?" Greta asked in astonishment.

"Yes."

"Then why not let me come every day to work while I am here — until the baby comes," Greta asked. "That is what I am — a servant. That is what I can do very well — work in a house. I came to England for that, but now I am doing nothing but waiting in a caravan for my baby to come. Your aunt would let me come to work for her?"

"At the usual rates," added Wally.

"I could ask her," said Jendy.

"Then ask her, please." Greta took the hand Wally held out, and moved away. "Please tell her that I am trained to work. I can come tomorrow, if she wants me. You will tell me what she says?"

"And remind her about the usual rates," called Wally.

The pompon rose and fell, and Jendy heard Allen's voice beside her.

"Well? What do you think of them?"

"Babes in the woods?" she suggested.

"Yes — and then again, no. That young fellow strikes me as being well able to get along. I've just been telling Roderick it was a bit risky to take him on without having seen him."

"Where did he come from?"

"Don't know. He turned up in the village and offered himself to a builder and got put on to one of the men working here — so Roderick said he'd employ him to do the clearing. Well, if he's no good, he can always throw him out."

"The girl — Greta — wants to work for Aunt Eddie."

"I dare say they can use the money. If Aunt Eddie doesn't want her, I'll tell Dan to give her a few light jobs around the house. They'll have to be light, judging from the imminence of the baby. Not married, as far as I could make out."

"No."

"Well, let me know what Aunt Eddie says."

It is not known what Aunt Eddie would have said if Jendy had merely relayed Greta's request. But with a cunning that surprised herself, she sought out Wally on the following morning and arranged that he should drive to Tallahouse when he had finished his day's work, and take Greta with him.

"I get the idea," he told Jendy with frank admiration. "I get out of the car and make the proposition to the old lady, and she turns it down flat, because for some reason she's taken a dislike to me. Then Greta steps out, the old lady sizes up the situation — and Greta gets the job. Right?"

"We hope she gets the job. How long," she asked, "has Greta been stepping out at just the right moment?"

"Round about two months," answered Wally, unabashed. "The first time, it was a bit of pure luck. Next time, I fixed it to see what happened. After that —"

"— it became routine."

" 'Sright. How is it you're so nice, even after being brought up by that old tiger? The tiger of Tallahouse."

"She isn't a tiger. She's perfectly reasonable when you get to know her. Will you bring Greta to see her?"

"You bet."

They arrived at about seven in the evening. They went to the back door, and Dolly, leaving them in the kitchen, went in search of Miss Latimer. Jendy, left in the drawing room, awaited with interest the result of the interview.

"I gather you've already seen this young couple," Aunt Eddie said on her return.

"Yes. I saw them when they came to the farm."

"Well, I don't like the young man's manner. I don't like it at all. When they first drove in here, I thought him extremely impertinent, and told him so. But the girl is quite different. He —"

"She said that she —"

"Will you not interrupt in the middle of a sentence? I was about to tell you that he didn't even remove that winter sports cap he was wearing. I stared at it to indicate that I expected him to remove it in my presence, and —"

"And did he?"

"If you'll wait until I've finished, you'll hear whether he did or not. He did. That is, he pretended that I was admiring it, and took it off to show it to me. Then he said that his wife was a maid by profession, and wanted to come and work here. Not that he put it that way. He merely said that his girl friend needed a job. I told him that I had long ago given up any hope of getting staff for a house of this kind, and explained that most of the rooms were closed and the furniture under dust sheets, and that the one maid I've got prefers to be left alone to do what she can. I was going to refuse the offer, when the girl happened to walk around the table and I saw to my astonishment that she was not only going to have a baby, but was going to have it within the next few weeks. I —"

"— said no?"

"Are you relating this incident," asked Aunt Eddie in exasperation, "or am I?"

"You are. But so slowly. All I'm doing is —"

"— prodding me on. Well, don't. You and Nancy — and your mother too, before you — always prod, prodding."

"Go on."

"I engaged the girl, of course. If she wants to do housework when she's in that condition, it must be because she needs the money. That's what comes of marrying a shiftless young man like that husband of hers."

Jendy, about to point out that no marriage had taken place, said nothing. Wally held unconventional views, but he also aired them freely. He was not above using Greta's condition to win over unsympathetic strangers, but it would not occur to him that his airy introduction could mislead anybody — or that they would care if it did. Aunt Eddie would learn the truth soon enough — and it would be interesting to be present when she learned it.

"She's coming at eleven tomorrow morning," went on Aunt Eddie. "Dolly says she'll give her a midday meal. The young man had the impertinence to point out that she should go back to the caravan to cook his dinner, but I soon told him what I thought of *that*."

There was an odd note in her voice. Her straight back was held ever more erect, and her eyes were full of a kind of grim anticipation. For the first time, Jendy realized that skirmishing had taken up a good deal of her aunt's life and had provided a large portion of its zest. It seemed almost a pity that Nature, having made her a bully, had surrounded her with victims who found an easy way of escape. Her brother Bertrand had used passive resistance. Dolly listened to orders and did just as she pleased. Nancy had laughed, and Jendy herself. . . .

Her own refuge, she realized, had been found at Farhills. She had lacked Nancy's ability to shrug off her aunt's brow-beating manner, and she had unconsciously taken the nearest escape route — and it had led her to the Harveys.

She studied her aunt with the clear gaze that her long absence from home seemed to have given her, and saw a lonely and disappointed old woman living in a doomed house, the last of her line, childless and by reason of her disposition almost friendless. She had taken in two orphan nieces, had mothered them in her own rough way, and they had gone away to lead lives far away from her. She was facing a lonely end — and facing it with a complete lack of self-pity.

After over twenty years, Jendy saw for the first time a person — a personality. And she liked what she saw.

"What are you staring at?" demanded the sharp voice.

"You."

"Well, don't. It's not polite. At my age, it isn't even kind. I'm an old hag and you never noticed it before — is that it?"

"Not quite. I was only thinking —"

"Well?"

"I was wishing I'd spent more time at home."

"And what would you have done here?"

"Got to know you better."

"No, you wouldn't. There's nearly fifty years' difference in our ages, and that's a gap that nothing can bridge. I belong to a world that's gone and you belong, God help you, to a new and far worse one. I've been fortunate, on the whole. I've had you and Nancy to make up for the children I never had — but I told myself, and kept on telling myself, that neither of you would ever care much for me — and I was right. I'm not complaining. I'm a sharp-tongued old woman and I like my own way and I was never a suitable companion for two pretty young girls. And now ring that bell and let's get dinner over."

"After dinner, can we have the box out?"

Aunt Eddie looked surprised.

"If you like."

The box was large, square and made of cardboard, and in it was a miscellaneous collection of papers, sketches, snapshots and photographs which for thirty years had waited to be sorted by Aunt Eddie. Jendy, in the past, had dreaded her aunt's command to fetch it from its place in the hall cupboard, and had endured long and boring evenings watching the contents being taken out, and listening to Aunt Eddie's acid comments on long-dead relatives. When a glance at the clock recalled her to the present, the papers, the photographs, still unsorted, would be bundled back into the box, and Jendy would carry it thankfully away.

But tonight she brought it out and sat watching with absorbed interest as Aunt Eddie went through it, and for the first time, a desire to learn something of her own past and her parents' past stirred in her. She sat with her chair drawn up to the littered card table, and helped to place the papers in appropriate piles, becoming acquainted as she did so with long-dead relations wearing feather boas or straw boaters or cycling bloomers or elaborate ball gowns, and learning of events which once had shattered the family peace, but no longer seemed to merit more than a passing attention: Great-Aunt Jendiss's insistence on marrying a man who was known to be dabbling in spiritualism, or maternal grandmother's indiscretion in engaging a music master who had taught her daughters everything but music.

"Who," asked Aunt Eddie irritably, diving deeper and deeper into the box, "wants to keep all these old photographs?"

"I do."

"You? Up to now, you've never shown the slightest interest in any of them."

"Up to now. — Who's this?"

"Your mother."

"That's not my father with her, is it?"

"It is not. He's one of the ones that got away."

"And who's this?"

"Your Uncle Bertrand — when he was young."

Jendy stared at the photograph.

"There isn't . . . there aren't any photographs of him anywhere in the house, are there?" she asked slowly.

"No."

"And he's the only one of the Latimers whose portrait isn't in the gallery." She looked at her aunt. "Did you . . . did you quarrel with him so badly that you —"

"— tried to obliterate his memory? No. That is," amended Aunt Eddie, "not quite." She took the photograph from Jendy and, looking at it, spoke in an almost absent tone. "It isn't easy to explain to you how I felt. You and Nancy have considered this house a sort of white elephant which has drained our resources, hung around our necks for generations and lost whatever touch of home and comfort it might once have had. You were brought up here, but it was never your home in the sense that it was mine and your mother's and your Uncle Bertrand's. We were born in it. The eldest son always died in it. You and Nancy never felt quite as I did, because tradition — family tradition — is something you have to have in your blood; something that gets into the blood when generation after generation of the same family have had their roots in one place — one house."

There was a pause; so long that she seemed to have finished.

"Go on," prompted Jendy softly.

"What's the use of going on? He's dead, and I can't make you understand. We never got on, he and I. I'm not easy to get on with; I admit it. I was older than he was, and perhaps I was a bully. Perhaps I got on his nerves unbearably, as he got older, harping on this theme of begetting an heir. I dare say I did — but I knew that he felt just as strongly about Tallahouse and the Latimer line as I did. And what I can't forgive him for . . ."

"Well?"

"That's wrong. One shouldn't bear grudges beyond the grave. But he should have married and had sons."

"Why isn't there a portrait of him in the gallery? Wasn't he ever painted?"

"Yes, he was. By a woman who lived at Ravenscroft for a time."

"And the picture wasn't hung?"

"No. For the simple reason that he died just after it was finished, and I didn't buy it."

"Why not?"

"Because . . . well, because his death was a shock in more ways than one. He'd been going over to Ravenscroft to sit for the portrait almost every day, and one day he came back, sat in his study by the fire, and when I went in to talk to him about something, I — I found his eyes closed. He looked asleep — but he wasn't sleeping. Or he was — forever. It's well over twenty years ago, but I can remember quite clearly what I felt as I stood looking at him, realizing that he was gone and that the line was at an end, and that perhaps I'd had something to do with bringing it to an end. If I'd left him alone, if I hadn't nagged him or badgered or bullied him to marry, if I hadn't irritated him by trying to find a wife for him, he would probably have done what any normal man would have done — found a wife for himself and had strong, sturdy children by her."

"Wasn't there ever anybody?"

"Never. My fault, I dare say. He was big and strong and, in his way, attractive. Women would have been glad . . . But he came to twenty years of age, twenty-five, thirty, thirty-five. . . . Perhaps he didn't realize that the years were slipping away. After he was forty-five, I lost heart. But in his study that day, I had a terrible feeling that perhaps he had found the only way he could of paying me out for my persistence. There he was — dead; dead without issue. And I saw us, the two of us, brother and sister, almost all their lives at loggerheads about one matter — an heir for Tallahouse. I felt I'd been more to blame than Bertrand. So I went around the house putting away things that reminded me . . . not of him, but of my own mistakes."

"But the portrait? Didn't you want to buy it?"

"I never saw it. I forgot about it for a time, and then the woman who painted it sent around a message to ask whether I wanted to buy it or not. She didn't come herself; she asked one of the tradesmen to ask me if I wanted the picture of Mr. Latimer. I thought the least she could have done was come herself. I didn't send any reply; I meant to go down when I felt a little better and take a look at it."

"And did you?"

"I did. But the house was closed, and she'd gone, taking all her pictures with her. One of these days, somebody'll walk past one of those London junkshops, and they'll see at the back of the window the portrait of the last Latimer of Tallahouse." She separated a sketch from the pile of papers and handed it to Jendy. "This was the preliminary sketch. I found it among your uncle's papers."

Jendy looked at it for a long time.

"What are the ships in the background?"

"The Armada. To make the connection, I suppose, between Talla and Drake."

"It's . . . it's good," Jendy said slowly, her eyes taking in details. "I like it."

"Yes, it's good. It's a good likeness, anyhow. I don't know whether that would

92

have come out so well on canvas."

"It's signed. At least, I think so, but I can't . . ."

"Luisa. That's what she called herself. Came from Brazil — so she said. I only saw her once, but she was wearing —"

"— red trousers."

"How do you know that?"

"Roderick Harvey was talking about her."

"Why in the world would Roderick Harvey be —"

"He was remembering some of the old tenants who'd lived at Ravenscroft. He said —"

But Aunt Eddie had looked at the clock, and was gathering up papers and putting them back into the box.

"Come along — bedtime," she said.

"Can I keep this sketch of Uncle Bertrand's portrait?"

"If you want to." Aunt Eddie tied up the box and rose to her feet. "And talking of odd tenants, the latest seem to be the oddest."

"Have you met them?"

"Not yet. Name of Peterson — Mr. and Mrs. When I say yet, I mean not formally. I ran into him in the village and I'd been hearing rumors that his wife suffered from a sort of kleptomania and I felt so sorry for him that I asked them to tea tomorrow. I'd like you to be here. They say she takes the silver and buries it, so you'd better be here to count the spoons. Now hurry up to bed — it's late."

They went upstairs together, and Jendy paused on the landing.

"Did Nancy," she asked, "ever mention some people called the Navarretes?"

"The who?"

"Navarretes. Spanish. Did she ever talk about them to you?"

"No. But I've heard the name."

"When?"

"Year or two ago. In connection with Roderick Harvey."

"With —?"

"Yes, that was it. I remember now. He was mixed up with a woman of that name. I'm not sure he wasn't engaged to her, but from the sound of it, she was no better than she should have been. There was a brother, too. He ran after Anabel Druce — and he didn't have to run far or run fast. The village was full of gossip at one time — they sounded a nasty lot, one way and another. I wouldn't expect Nancy to mention them — unless her standards have fallen very considerably. Did you think she knew them?"

"I wasn't sure."

Aunt Eddie seemed to be waiting for more, but Jendy had no more to say. She went slowly to her room, thinking of Anabel and the man called Carlos, and Roderick Harvey and the sister . . . what was her name? Milagros. Miracle. He had been engaged to her. But he had said nothing about that. He had said nothing of himself in connection with Milagros; he had only hinted that Nancy. . . .

And she had listened to him, and had left him without leaving the imprint of her hand on his dark, handsome, unreadable face.

And that was another miracle.

CHAPTER 4

On passing Gannets on her way to the farm
the next morning, Jendy heard the loud
closing of the front door, followed by
footsteps going down the paved forecourt to
the gate. She braced herself to meet Anabel,
and experienced the same sensation of min-
gled fear and fascination that the sight of her
had roused throughout her childhood.

A meeting, she knew, would have to come.
Sooner or later, they must come across one
another at the farm, or on the way to the
farm, since they both spent most of their
time there. It must come, and she must try
to parry, as she had had to do in the past,
the other woman's vindictive thrusts. There
was no Nancy now to give blow for blow —
and in the old days, she remembered, the
blows had frequently been more than verbal.

She found it difficult to decide what had

been at the root of Anabel's hatred of Nancy — and to a lesser degree, herself. Some of it had perhaps been, as Aunt Eddie had said, jealousy — jealousy of Nancy, whose looks and attractions had in those old days outweighed Anabel's. But there had been something more: a mutual loathing that sprang from their unbridgable divergence of views on almost every subject. She and Nancy had learned very early in life that their moral standards — modeled upon Aunt Eddie's — were completely opposed to Anabel's; and they had discovered that she considered them out of date, totally unrealistic, and prudish to a ludicrous degree. She had laughed at them — and the laughter had been hard to bear.

But it was not Anabel who arrived at the gate at the same moment as Jendy. It was a girl of about eight, and Jendy, realizing that she must be Anabel's daughter Beulah, abandoned at the first glimpse of her the image that had grown up in her mind of a sad-eyed little creature torn and bewildered by her mother's frequent divorces. This child was fat, sleek, and completely, insolently at ease. Her hair was dark, and worn in two plaits which reached to her shoulders. She was bareheaded, and had on a serviceable brown raincoat; on her feet were short rubber boots. She had a freckled skin, a snub nose, large teeth with a gap in front, and mean little boldly staring eyes.

"Hello," she said casually, as she came out of the gateway. "I suppose you're Jendy?"

"Yes. You must be Beulah."

"M'm." Beulah fell into step, fished in her pockets and brought out a bag of sweets. Without offering them to Jendy, she began to eat them.

"Going down to Farhills?" she enquired laconically, between sucks.

"Yes. Are you?"

"Yes. I go every day. Allen likes me to go — he said so. I help him with the animals, and everything. I know him better than you do, I expect."

"Perhaps you do," Jendy said mildly. "These aren't holidays, are they? Shouldn't you be at school?"

"We've got quarantine. Mumps." Beulah produced two battered squares of chocolate, peeled off the silver paper and threw it carelessly on to the road. "My last stepfather was Spanish — did you know?"

"I'd heard."

"I'm glad my mother got sick of him. I

did, too. He was a scream. His name was . . . guess what? Adolpho. The only thing was, he used to come to England a lot, and he took me to London lots of times. We went to theaters, and I stopped up late at night — later than any of the other girls at school. I nearly didn't go back to school; I thought I'd like to be an actress, because I'm good at acting; everybody says so. I could be famous if I wanted to."

"Really?"

"But I don't know whether I'd like to just act, or to dance and sing. I can dance and sing jolly well, so I might do that — but the teachers at my school would be sorry, because they told me I was too good at lessons to stop going to school. They said I could be top if I wanted to. They said they liked teaching me much more than they liked teaching the other girls, because I was clever. I asked the teachers to come to London with me, and I took them to —"

"But weren't they teaching their classes?"

"It was a holiday," said Beulah without the slightest hesitation. "The other girls were jolly jealous, but I didn't care. Are you jealous of people?"

"I don't think so."

"My mother said you were jealous of her

99

when she lived here before. You and your sister — the one who's called Nancy. She's gone away, hasn't she?"

"Yes."

"My mother says she doesn't blame her, because living on a farm isn't as exciting as Spain, and she said she could've told Allen, if he'd asked her. I went to Spain, and I went into a bull ring and I got a cape and waved it at the bull, all by myself. Then —"

"Pass the salt."

"Then I . . . What did you say?"

"Nothing."

"Oh. Well, now I'm going to stay here for a long, long time because my mother's going to, and I'm going to do a lot of helping on the farm. I can even born a calf if I want to, and I could cut off the sheep's wool, only there aren't any sheep. Once I went to a sheep farm."

"Whereabouts?"

This time, Beulah had to pause; the choice was wide.

"Australia," she selected. "Have you been there?"

"No."

"It's got kangaroos. I bought a lot, and I kept them and tamed them."

"Did you buy any aborigines?"

"No, because I'd spent all my money on the kangaroos and . . . You're walking awfully fast."

Jendy walked even faster. She liked children, but she could not like this one. She could allow for a little stretching of imagination, but there was something about Beulah's smugly delivered lies that she found distasteful. Fat, greedy and lying were not adjectives she ever remembered applying to a child before, but this one seemed to merit them. She tried to make herself believe that the greed and the lies might be the result of insecurity of background — but there was nothing insecure about Anabel's background, and Jendy remembered, with a clarity that brought back all the dislike she felt for her, Anabel's greed, Anabel's lies. But she had been more cunning than her daughter — and infinitely more subtle.

The farm was in sight. At the gates, Beulah turned and left her, going toward the building site — and Jendy, following the fat, stocky figure, looked beyond it and saw in the distance the tall, slim figure of Anabel.

So she was here. That was good, for she would keep Roderick Harvey to herself — and she was welcome to him. The farther away and the longer she kept him, the more peaceful hours there would be with Allen.

She walked across the yard and made her way to the orchard, where she could see Allen examining a leaking water trough. The day was rough and windy, and she had tied a scarf around her head, and as she came toward him, he thought with a stab of pain that she looked like Nancy. On an impulse, he told her so.

"With my hair hidden, you mean?" she asked.

"Yes. You've got the same-shaped face as she has — I'd never noticed it before. — Don't walk too near that bit of ground; it's soaked and you'll sink into it."

"I walked here with Beulah."

"Nice for you. Anabel's here — up at the site, with Roderick."

"I caught a glimpse of her."

"She went by me without a word or a look. I honestly think she didn't see me — she looked like a huntress ready for the kill."

Jendy looked at him.

"You sound as though you thought it was serious," she said.

"It is serious — for Roderick."

"Does he . . . like her?"

"No. But that won't save him from getting

102

sucked in if he lets himself get drawn too close. I'm not really worrying; he's pretty good at taking care of himself."

She was staring up at the two distant figures.

"Country sports," she said.

"What was that?"

"I said country sports. What she's wearing."

"Well" — he turned an amused glance on her — "you always knew she was dressy. What did you think of Beulah?"

Jendy smiled.

"Not exactly a case for a psychiatrist, is she? I'd pictured her as one of those Henry James characters — a mass of complexities; introspective and —"

"— doing her best to unite her parents? Not Beulah. Her own father faded out of the picture long ago, and I think her stepfathers all went out of their way to make themselves agreeable."

"Which makes sense. I never really believed in Mr. Murdstone — did you? I used to skip all the bits about him because they irritated me. Wouldn't he have known that the quickest way to his wife's heart, and the peace of the home, would have been to get her son on his side? — What does Beulah do here? Wander around as Nancy and I used to?"

"She doesn't keep out of trouble as you two did. She's a mean child; she spies on the men and comes and tells tales — or tries to. I'd throw her off the place if I hadn't an ineradicable feeling that no child could really be as bad as she seems to be. But she does know that if she gives any real trouble, I'll put her out and keep her out — and that seems to act as a brake."

They were walking toward the yard, and Jendy saw Wally Booth's black car approaching the gate. Leaving Allen, she went to speak to him.

"Took Greta up to your aunt's house," he said, getting out. "Going to fetch her this evening." He jerked his head in the direction of the building site. "Seen the lady visitor?"

"Yes."

"Know her?"

"Yes."

"Lucky you. She never gives me a look. I'm only the fellow who's clearing the ground that's going to be the garden she's busy planning — for herself. If she'd only give me her attention for a minute, I'd tell her that she isn't going to find it as easy as all that."

"Why not?"

"You know quite well," Wally said calmly. "You understand all right. You know as well as I do that my boss is an old hand at dealing with women. Women that go after him, I mean. It's going to be a pleasure to watch."

The words were impertinent, but his manner so easy, so natural and so buoyant that she found it impossible to take offense.

"You can't be getting much work done," she remarked.

"Care to come up and see?"

She nodded, and they walked down the road for a few yards and then he led her through a wide gap that the builders had made in the hedge bordering the road, in order to tip truck-loads of material near the site.

"Mind your ankles," he warned. "Loose stone. Up this way."

He put out a hand and pulled her up the last steep yards.

"There!" he said.

He had indeed, she saw, made some impression on the tangle of overgrowth. There was a neat, wide area of clearance, and she stood looking at it and trying to visualize the colorful flowerbeds that one day would bloom here. For Roderick Harvey —

and perhaps for Anabel.

Above, but out of sight behind the screen of trees, were the builders. She could hear Roderick's voice, and Anabel's saying something in reply — and then her attention went to Wally, who had given an angry exclamation.

"Hey — take a look up there," he said.

He was staring up at the branches of a tree. Jendy, following his glance, caught a glimpse of Beulah's fat legs.

"Come down here, you," ordered Wally.

The leaves parted, and Beulah peered down.

"Why?"

"Come down first and ask why afterward," directed Wally.

His voice had lost its drawl, and there was a note in it which made Beulah study him with more attention.

"Shan't," she said at last. "You're only one of the workmen and you can't tell me what to do."

"I'm not one of the workmen. On this job, I'm the only workman," he told her. "And I'm not going to have you sitting up there. Are you coming down, or do I start throwing stones?"

"If you do, I'll tell my mother."

"Me, too. I'll tell her," said Wally. "I'll tell her plenty — about you. I'll count five. One, two —"

Somewhat to Jendy's surprise, Beulah's face disappeared, and a moment later her legs began to wave in the air, seeking a branch. She began her descent, coming down clumsily but steadily, and stood before them at last in her rumpled mackintosh, her face red with anger.

"I don't see why I have to do anything you tell me to," she said shrilly to Wally. "I was just sitting up there, that's all."

"What for?"

"I was looking at those people, and they were funny."

"What people?"

"The Petersons. They're the people who live in that house next door called Ravenscroft, and if you climb up, you can see into their garden."

"And what's so funny?"

"They are. I mean, *she* is. She's potty. She buries things in the garden and then he goes out and digs them up. I've been watching them. I think it's funny, and you've got no —"

"Spying!"

"I wasn't spying! I was just looking, that's

all, and I'm going to tell Mr. Harvey about you."

"That's right; go ahead and tell him. And I'll tell you something: if I catch you up one of those trees again, snooping, I'll fetch you down personally, and you'll get down faster than you got up."

"I'll jolly well climb up every time I want to," yelled Beulah. "I will! It's not your farm! It's Mr. Harvey's, and he'll let me."

"Want to bet?"

Beulah aimed a kick at him.

"You mind your own beastly business," she shouted. "Who d'you think you are, anyway?"

"That's enough of that," put in Jendy. "You had no business to be up there looking at the Petersons. It was mean."

"It wasn't mean! They didn't even know I was there!"

"What" — it was Roderick's voice speaking from a ledge above them — "is all this about?"

"Where's my Mummy?" demanded Beulah. "That man over there —"

"Your mother's on her way home and so are you," Roderick broke in. "Off you go."

"I want to climb trees. Why can't I, just because he says I can't?"

"If he says you can't, you can't. Goodbye."

Beulah stared at him, saw something in his expression that she did not care for, kicked some stones angrily out of her way, and departed.

"Up a tree, spying on the neighbors," explained Wally. "Do they really dig?"

"They say so in the village," said Roderick. "Next time our fat little friend goes up to take a look, you can haul her along to me."

"I can take care of her," said Wally coolly. "My Mum knew how to keep kids in order, and I got the knack from her. And now, if you'll excuse me, I'll go on earning my pay envelope."

It was so calm, so clear a dismissal that Jendy found herself accepting Roderick's help in pulling her up the slope toward his house. They skirted it and went down the path toward the farm.

"I'm going in to have a drink — nice cool beer," he said as they neared the farmhouse. "Coming?"

"No, thanks. I've got to go back fairly soon."

He glanced down at her with amusement written plainly on his face.

"Angry?" he asked.

"No." Her voice was cool. "Not at

all angry."

"Then there's no reason why you shouldn't come in and have a drink — or watch me while I drink. You're going to see a lot of me if you're going to be here for some time — and you can't go on looking at me as though I'd made dishonorable proposals to you — or something. Let's be friends."

She hesitated, and then common sense told her that it would be better to establish once and for all a relationship between them that would have all the outward appearances of friendship. She would be pleasant, and cool — and wary.

"Thank you; I'd like a drink," she said.

"That's better. Come on."

He took her into the dim, cool drawing room and settled her in a low chair. Then he brought her a drink and stood looking down at her with his own glass in his hand.

"To friendship," he said.

"To friendship," she agreed.

"No more rows."

"No more rows," she agreed.

"Then we'd better keep off the subject of Nancy," he said coolly.

"Yes, we'd better. But Aunt Eddie —" she began, and stopped.

"Aunt Eddie?" he prompted.

"She said that it was you who . . . who first told Nancy —"

"— to get out of here? That's true."

"Then how can you blame her for going away? You, of all people. You yourself —"

"— got out and stayed out? True again. What's that line? 'What do they know of England who only England know?' or words to that effect. I'm an artist — of a sort. I needed change and stimulus and color and drama — so I went looking for them. As you get older, you mellow — or you should. I see this place with different eyes now, but when I was younger, I felt it lacked something. And then one day, I came home on a visit. It was spring. Nancy was here, and she was twenty-five, beautiful, intelligent, sensitive — and all she knew, all she'd ever seen, was this." He waved a hand. "I'd never seen so lovely a woman in so small a setting before, and it seemed to me all wrong. So I talked to her. I told her to get away and see things — new things, new places, new people. I showed her color slides of my old studio in Madrid, its outside walls hidden, its windows half hidden behind flowers. I told her to go — and she went. She rented the studio, and when I went over to Spain, I put her in touch with several people I knew.

But I didn't tell her to stay there forever, or to get things out of focus, or to lose her bearings. Or to lose her head. At twenty-five, with her sound upbringing, who would have supposed that she'd take the Navarretes seriously?"

"You took them seriously." The words were out before Jendy could stop them. "You were engaged to her — weren't you?"

He did not answer. He was staring at her, and she thought that his face had grown pale.

"Where on earth," he asked slowly, "did you hear that?"

"Aunt Eddie wasn't sure, but —"

"— but she was willing to pass on what she didn't know. For sheer malice," he asked in wonder, "can you beat a remote little Godforsaken village like this one?"

"Was it only gossip?"

"Not entirely. But how in the world the news got through to . . . Ah! Anabel, of course."

"Was she out there?"

"Not at the time. She went out later, when she married her third husband. They lived in Madrid, and she met Milagros and got the version that Milagros was putting out. And brought it back to England. With your Aunt

Eddie to sketch in my past for you, I'm not surprised you look at me with that lie-down-dog expression. It frightens me — you know why?"

"No."

"Because I'm afraid of driving you away from the farm. You're needed here. If you refused to come and see Allen . . ."

"You couldn't make me do that."

"No? I'm glad to hear it." He raised his glass again. "To friendship — for Allen's sake." he took a step nearer, and his next words were spoken soberly. "Be kind to him, Jendy. Next to myself and Nancy, you're the person I think he thinks most of in the world."

Next to Nancy. . . .

To her horror, she felt tears pricking her eyes. She got up hastily and walked to the window and stood with her back to him, speaking unsteadily.

"I'd give anything . . . anything. . . ."

"I know you would." He was standing behind her, his hands on her shoulders. "But why do you let it worry you so much? She's gone, but she may come back. God knows I'm no prophet, but somehow I can't rid myself of the feeling that she'll end up here — with Allen. People can't always learn lessons about themselves the easy way. I didn't, for one. I thought I could uproot myself, and I found I couldn't. Perhaps Nancy'll find that, too."

She dried her eyes and turned.

"I'm sorry," she said. "I don't know what made me . . ."

"This room," he said. "She's in most places on the farm, but in this room, she comes back to me more than anywhere else. You may feel that too, so when you come in here, your guard comes down."

She walked to the fireplace and rested her forehead against the mantelpiece.

"What you said about her coming back —" she began.

"Do you feel it too?"

"Not in the way you do. But the thing I remember is how happy she used to be here."

"I didn't know enough about her in old days," Roderick said. "It wasn't until I came home two years ago that I got to know her — and got to thinking she was wasting her time here. All I wanted her to do was see a little of the world before marrying Allen and settling down. She wasn't interested — at first. She even recited poetry to make me see how she felt about living here."

"Rupert Brooke."

"Yes. How do you know?"

"Because she used to say the lines to me:

'Stands the Church clock at ten to
    three
  And is there honey still for tea.' "

"No. They weren't the ones.

'A body of England's breathing
    English air
  Washed by the rivers, blest by sun of
    home.' "

he quoted softly. "Those two lines used to come back to me again and again and again. Perhaps, in the end, they brought me home. And it's because Nancy felt that way that I don't believe she'll stay away forever."

"Sometimes at night," said Jendy slowly, "when I'm thinking about her, I don't believe she'll stay away forever, either. So I go on hoping."

He said nothing for some time. His eyes were on her, brooding, speculative. She looked up at him questioningly at last, and he spoke quietly.

"I go on hoping too," he said.

CHAPTER 5

The Petersons were to come to tea at Tallahouse at half past four that afternoon, but shortly after lunch, as Jendy was trying to clear some of the weeds from the drive, a car drove up, and from it alighted a thickset, bald-headed, aggressive-looking man of about fifty. He informed Jendy in an abrupt manner and in a strong Northern accent that his name was Peterson and that he had called to see Miss Latimer.

She led him into the drawing room and sent Dolly in search of her aunt. Having invited Mr. Peterson to sit down, she made a polite attempt to engage him in conversation as they waited, but the visitor, clearly disinclined for small talk, merely stared out of the window and drummed his fingers impatiently on his knee.

On Aunt Eddie's entrance, he rose and at

once stated his reason for calling.

"Shan't keep you long," he said. "Came round because there's something I've always got to explain before anybody meets Mrs. Peterson — my wife. I've come along to warn you that she's got a bit of a, as you might say, peculiarity."

"What sort?" asked Aunt Eddie.

"She buries things. Our own things, mostly, but at times other folk's. And that's where the awkwardness comes in."

He spoke brusquely; Jendy thought that he also spoke mechanically, as though he had made this explanation many times before and it had become routine.

"What sort of things does she bury?" asked Aunt Eddie.

"All sorts — small, mostly. Bits of silver, bits of brass, ornaments and suchlike. It's been going on for years. She was out in Burma before she married me, and when the Japs moved in, she buried everything she could lay her hands on. I suppose that started her off, but when I married her, she was quite O.K. Then she began to be a bit queer — difficult time of life, I dare say — and whether it's anything to do with that old business, I can't tell you; but every now and then she seems to get the idea that the Japs are on the way, and she takes something out and buries it. You might, or you might not, find her taking a look at some of your things. If she does, take no notice. Take no notice at all. I can deal with it."

There was a short silence. Aunt Eddie, for once, seemed to have no comment to make, and Mr. Peterson's flat statement seemed designed to rule out sympathy. She was about to thank him for coming to explain the matter, and say that he and his wife would be welcome when they called later in the afternoon, when he embarked upon a different topic.

"D'you know anything about a fat little girl who lives hereabouts?" he asked. "Wears a brown mackintosh and wanders round that farm next door to us — what's it called? Farhills."

"You must mean Beulah," Aunt Eddie said. "She's the daughter of —"

"I know all about her mother," broke in Mr. Peterson. "She passed us once or twice in that flashy car of hers, and my wife recognized her from the pictures in the papers. Just divorced, and not for the first time. Where's she staying?"

"With her brother, Mr. Druce, who lives at Gannets."

"Gannets? That's the house —"

"— less than a mile from this one. It stands almost on the road, with a little courtyard in front."

"I know it. I know that chap Druce, too. If you call him a chap. Goes shopping in the village carrying a big canvas bag with flowers embroidered all over it — that's him, isn't it?"

"He's a very quiet neighbor, and he doesn't offend anybody," Aunt Eddie said.

Her tone implied that the same could not be said of some other neighbors, but Mr. Peterson was too much occupied with his own problems to notice shades of tone.

"Mother who's no good, uncle who ought to be in petticoats. Isn't there anybody else — anybody responsible — who looks after the child?"

"Not as far as I know," said Aunt Eddie.

"Well, I'll have to speak to mother and uncle. But if you've got any influence, I'd be glad if —"

"What have you got against Beulah?" asked Aunt Eddie.

"Trespass. She's been in my garden once or twice, and I shoved her out — and then she took to climbing trees. She gets up those trees that overlook our house, and she sits up there staring into our garden. When I spotted her, I knew who it was who'd been spreading tales about my wife round the village. Nobody else could've known about her. Nobody'd asked us to visit them, and we'd asked nobody to visit us. We don't keep servants, and we don't have tradesmen calling at the door. That way, I hoped we'd be able to keep our affairs to ourselves — but when I went down to the village, what happened? Whispers. Nudges. Stares. And a gossiping old crone asks me if my wife's recovering from a breakdown. See what I mean? All because a kid who's out of control and who needs her seat warmed spreads stories about us. I want her kept out of those trees."

"I'm sorry," said Aunt Eddie, "but there's really nothing I can do. The child hasn't lived here; her mother used to come down sometimes when the old people were alive, but after they died, the only time she came was to settle up their affairs — and so I know very little about Beulah. I keep her out of here because I know she's trouble-some."

"In my place, what would you do?" demanded Mr. Peterson. "I take a barn of a place and pay a rent out of all proportion just to get privacy. And then I don't get it. Well, a kid of eight or nine isn't going to do me out of something I'm paying good money for. If the people responsible for her won't do anything, I'll take matters into my own hands."

He rose and took an abrupt leave, and Aunt Eddie looked after him thoughtfully.

"Interesting world," she said. "He talked about privacy, but who gets any nowadays? There was a time when I could have arranged to keep the Mr. Petersons out of my drawing room."

"But you asked them to tea," pointed out Jendy.

"That was because I felt sorry for them. But in my young days, nobody got in unless we wanted them to. Just a simple statement to the effect that one wasn't at home. But nowadays, I'm summoned to every trades-man's dispute, and I'm brought down to meet every stranger who imagines I live here merely to show them round. — It's sad, isn't it, that one can't summon up any sympathy for Beulah? If it were any other child, the thought of that man threatening her would be dreadful."

"Perhaps he'll chase her up trees. Didn't Dolly's old aunt take to burying things?"

"Yes. But she hadn't any silver to bury, so she used to go up to the Oxterley Arms and try to make off with the pewter tankards. But there's a lot to this burying. Your Uncle Bertrand bought a lot of old china — valuable old china — from an antique dealer. I told him time and time again that it wasn't valuable and it wasn't old, but would he listen? No. Then the police caught up with the dealer, and it turned out that he'd made a fortune by buying new china cheap, and then cracking it and burying it and digging it up again as genuinely antique. I can't tell you what sums your uncle had spent by that time. I tried to keep some of the stuff in the house, just to remind him what a fool he'd been, but he managed to get rid of it behind my back. — Have you been along to see how Greta's getting on?"

"No. I'll go now."

"And I'll come with you, to see that you don't keep her talking too long, wasting her time — and my money."

They found Greta in the huge kitchen, said to have been designed by Jendiss Talla herself. The massive fireplace, the two spits and the enormous trestle table suggested that she had anticipated some of the problems of catering for fourteen-in-family, as well as for innumerable serving men and maids. At one end of the table, Greta was mixing scones.

"Dolly," she explained, as Jendy and her aunt came in, "said that I must not wash windows — and so I am doing the things for tea."

She was wearing a patched, pale blue overall the exact color of her eyes. Her hair was hidden under a tightly bound yellow duster, and her sleeves were pushed above her rounded elbows. She looked as clean, as fresh and as beguiling as a baby straight from its bath.

"Dolly was quite right," said Aunt Eddie. "I told her you weren't to do anything heavy. There's plenty to be done besides window-washing."

"Then why don't you let me bring Wally inside when he comes to fetch me this evening?" Greta opened the oven and inserted a batch of scones. "He is very strong, and he can do the heavy things."

"After his own day's work, you should take your husband home and give him a good, hot meal," said Aunt Eddie. "That's what wives are for."

"I am not yet a wife," said Greta, reaching for the flour bin, "but when I am, I hope that there will be a nice house for him to go home to. But please let him come and work here. He will enjoy it."

"In that case," began Aunt Eddie, "he can —"

Then, as the significance of Greta's words penetrated her mind, she stopped abruptly. For some time she stood with her eyes fixed incredulously on the girl, who, busy and unconscious of tension, was mixing more scones.

"You said . . . You said . . ." Aunt Eddie brought out at last. "Did I understand you to say that you are not . . ."

Greta looked at her.

"Oh, you thought that Wally and I were married? At first, that is what everybody thinks."

Aunt Eddie was looking at Jendy.

"You knew?"

"Oh yes, Jendy knew," said Greta. "If she did not say it to you, it was perhaps because she thought that you would be shocked. You are shocked?"

"Shocked?" Aunt Eddie made the word sound four syllables long. "Shocked? I am speechless. You mean to tell me, calmly and without any sign of anxiety, to say nothing of regret, that you are bearing the child of a man to whom you are not married?"

"Yes, you are shocked," Greta said. "People who are older do not like that I am not married. They —"

"Sit down," ordered Aunt Eddie.

Greta sat down and folded her hands on her lap.

"Now pay attention to me. How old are you?"

"I am twenty years."

"And you came to this country —"

"— to work, and for my English. And I met Wally. He and I were working for the same man, and —"

"— and you are now living together in a caravan. So far, I am not concerned with the matter. Your morals, even if you have none, are your own affair. But you are now in my employment, and you have just proposed that your hus — your young man shall work in this house in the evenings. Do you imagine for one moment that I would allow him to do so, knowing that he is depriving you and your child of security, depriving you of any legal claim to him or to his aid, depriving your baby even of a name?"

"Of course," Greta assured her, " we shall marry. We mean to marry. It is only that other things have come in the way of it, and —"

"Other things? *Other* things? Are there any other things more important than the future of your child?"

"Nothing, no," agreed Greta. "But we have put it off and —"

"Who did the putting-off?" Aunt Eddie inquired, her brow black with suspicion. "*He* did, I take it?"

"Wally? No, not Wally. Me, for most of the time. He said to get married, and I said yes, but we were not settled in one place, and I said we should wait until . . . But we shall get married, of course."

"If I have anything to do with it, you most certainly will," Aunt Eddie promised grimly. "Don't imagine for one moment that I am going to stand by and see a pretty, sensible young girl like you bringing a child into this world without a name. When this young man comes this evening, you will kindly tell him that I wish to see him at once."

She marched out of the room, her face red with anger. After a few moments, Greta spoke in the calm way that characterized her.

"She thinks that Wally is wicked, your aunt."

"Not wicked; just a bit on the casual side."

"She thinks he has no rules, perhaps

126

even no religion."

"Has he?"

"In his own way, yes. He is religious, in his way, more than I am. He likes to go to church — any church, it does not matter which. He says that Heaven will only have one gate for everybody."

"I'm sure he's right. Don't you want to be married?"

"Yes, of course. There is time, you know."

"Not much time."

"Enough time. We will do it one day — you will see. And then your aunt will be happy."

Jendy pulled out a chair and sat at the table beside the younger girl.

"When did you two meet?" she asked.

"Wally and I? When I came to England two years ago. He was working with the same man that I was working with in London — only I was the housekeeper, the maid, working in the house, and Wally was working somewhere else, in the office. One day —"

"The office?"

"Yes. He was in an office, but he did not like it. He did not like to work inside, and he is glad now that he has got work outside — work with his hands, which he says are strong, instead of work with his head, which he says is weak. One day, he came from the office to the house with some papers, and I opened the door, and from that moment we were in love. You see?"

Jendy saw. The London house, the knock on the door. Wally on the doorstep, papers in hand. Wally, in clothes less colorful than the ones he now wore; dark hair, handsome, happy face, clear and carefree eyes. The door opening to reveal this pink-and-white-and-golden girl . . .

"Yes, I see," she said.

"He asked me who I was, and I told him that I had come to work as a servant and to learn English — my English was not much then. He said, afterward, that he thought I was like sunshine. He meant because the hall was dark and the day was foggy and everything was rather dull —"

"— and there you were, with golden hair and milk-white skin."

"Not white at all. I came in the winter, and I had of course been on skis all the time at my home. I was tanned by the sun — brown."

"Did he have as devastating an effect on you?"

"In a way. I was so glad, you can't understand how glad, to see a young person.

In the house was only an old man. At the classes I went to were young people, but like me, they had to work and could not come to visit me. It is not easy to make friends in this country. It is easy to meet people here and there, but they are sometimes not interesting, not gay. Wally and I loved each other right away."

"And then?"

"Then we began to go out a little, and then more, and we thought that one day we might be married. And you know how it is, he came one evening, and we were alone, and then before we knew, there was the baby."

"Were you glad?"

"Oh yes, very glad. Perhaps in Sweden we think a little differently about these things. But I am glad, and Wally is glad. This is a baby which will be born from love, and we think that is beautiful."

"But from the purely protective angle — the security angle my aunt was talking about? Doesn't it worry you that the baby —"

"We shall be married — you will see. One day, it will happen suddenly." She rose and began to set a tray with tea things, and glanced curiously at Jendy. "You are not like your aunt," she said slowly, "but all the same, I think that you would not have done as I did. Would you?"

Jendy hesitated.

"Probably not," she said at last.

"You think marriage first — love after?"

"I think that everybody has the right to act the way they want to — what's called according to their lights."

"But for yourself?"

"For myself . . . I've never really worked it out. Nobody ever put the proposition up to me."

"And if they had? If they did?"

Jendy gazed at her own reflection in the side of the silver teapot.

"I feel a bit more strongly about marriage than you and Wally seem to do," she said slowly. "I like it as an institution. I've probably got highly romantic ideas about it. I think of myself at times as a wife and mother, but always in what I feel is a nice secure framework. Perhaps being brought up in a house like this gives one a sort of special regard for permanent things. If you call marriage a permanent thing. Some people don't."

She thought of Anabel, who made nonsense of marriage vows. She was still thinking of her when she left the kitchen — and as she reached the hall, she was still too deep in musing to be able to take the usual evasive action at the sight of Milford Druce.

He was obviously in search of her, and as she usually saw to it that he searched without finding, she was a little ashamed at the delight that overspread his face when he saw her.

"Jendy — my dear Jendy!" He came toward her with hands outstretched, his eyes gleaming with joy behind rimless glasses. "I can't believe you're really here to stay!"

She led him into the drawing room, resolved to be more patient with his little eccentricities. He was dull, and slightly ridiculous, but he was kind — and harmless. He had been the first man who had ever paid more attention — more attentions — to herself than to Nancy. It had been a tepid courtship, an even more tepid proposal, and he had looked relieved at her refusal. Then, as though he had done as much as could be expected of him to prove his manhood, he had settled down to contented spinsterhood, his life divided between cooking, feeding his birds and animals and tending the beautiful goldfish in the pond in his little formal garden. With a quiet old couple to work for him and an occasional visitor to lunch or to dinner, he had been going along in happy tranquility — until his sister's unheralded arrival. The eagle swooping on the dove, Jendy thought — and resolved once more to be kind.

"Let's go and sit in the garden," she suggested. "It's a shame to stay indoors and waste the sunshine."

He followed her out, but his spirits had sunk, and she had no difficulty in deciding what was on his mind. He had come to unburden himself — and this time, she would lend a sympathetic ear.

He did not come at once to the point. One of the things she liked about him was his unfailing discovery of beauty where others missed it. She saw only a garden seat half lost in tall weeds that also hid what had once been a lovely rose garden. Milford, parting the tall grasses, bent down to rescue, to bring to light, a rose struggling to make itself seen.

"Look," he murmured tenderly. "So lovely, and so lost. Come and look, Jendy."

She walked to his side and looked at the pale pink flower. Beside her, Milford seemed to be purring.

"I love best of all the hybrid tea roses," he said, straightening. "Don't you?"

"I'm ashamed to say I don't know much
. . ."

"Nothing, nothing can match their color.
There's one here. . . . No. I thought, I
hoped it might be one of the hybrid
polyanthas." He sighed. "Can't anything be
done, Jendy dear, to make this garden what
it used to be?"

"Aunt Eddie can't work in a garden any
more, and you know how she is about
gardeners," she said. "She expects them to
clear the entire place in a week, as well as
plant vegetable gardens and produce what
she calls flowers. So they won't come. More
accurately, they won't stay."

"It's such a pity. My father used to love
this rose garden. There's a rose here —
somewhere, if one could only find it — that
he planted himself. It was called Frau Karl
Druschki. Wasn't that a sweet name? I used
to think of the Frau as a busy housewife,
cooking great dishes for Karl — but then it
seemed to me that perhaps that wasn't the
right picture of somebody who had had a
rose — a lovely rose — named after her. So
I put her into an elegant little salon and . . .
Look, Jendy dear — another poor little bush
struggling here. Isn't it curious that roses
did so well in your garden, and so badly in

ours? My father was always getting experts down, but nothing came of it — and that's why I've never attempted to grow roses."

"Come and sit down and I'll see about clearing all the weeds away later," she said. "Why don't you stay to tea? The Petersons are coming."

He looked at her with surprise and apprehension.

"Petersons? Not the Ravenscroft tenants?"

"Yes."

His face grew pale, his manner flustered.

"Oh dear, oh dear! I wouldn't have dreamed that your aunt would have met . . . would have invited . . ."

"She felt a little sorry for them, and asked them to come to tea."

"*Sorry* for them?"

"Mrs. Peterson appears to have some kind of kleptomania. He came and told us about it."

"He came here?"

"Yes."

"He didn't by any chance . . . I mean, he didn't mention Beulah, did he?"

"Yes, he did."

Milford took out a large handkerchief, and for a moment Jendy thought he was going to burst into tears. But it was only to wipe his brow.

"There's some . . . some unpleasantness," he quavered. "This man — Mr. Peterson — came to see me just before lunch. No, it wasn't before lunch; it was after lunch. . . . I feel so confused . . ."

"Did you talk to him?"

"Talk to him?" His voice squeaked with surprise. "*Talk* to him? Jendy dear, you can't know what sort of fellow he is. He's . . . he's most aggressive. Most. I've seen him in the village, and he . . . he *eyed* me. In the most sinister way. He's not at all the sort of person I would have imagined your aunt would have to tea. From what I gathered in the village, he appears to think that I have some kind of responsibility for Beulah. But I haven't! She's . . . I've no responsibility for her at all!"

"Didn't you tell Mr. Peterson so?"

"Tell him? I haven't seen him."

"But you said —"

"Yes, he came. But I recognized his car. Most, most fortunately. I happened to be at a window when the car stopped outside the house. Naturally, I went out. I went out the other way, and I didn't come back until I was sure . . ."

"But he's bound to run you to earth some

time, isn't he?" asked Jendy, and regretted the unfortunate words when she saw the last vestige of color drain out of Milford's cheeks. "Anabel's the one he wants?" she added consolingly.

"Of course! But you know what she is, Jendy! She laughs at any protests about her own behavior — or Beulah's. I don't want to speak ill of a child, but that child is a . . . a little monster. Mr. and Mrs. Duke told me today tht if she doesn't go, they'll have to. And I've had them so long, and they're so quiet, and they know so *exactly* how I like things to be done. . . . Tell me what I can do!"

"Couldn't you tell Anabel that you're in danger of losing your staff? It would make a difference to her comfort as well as yours."

"She'd only laugh. She's . . . It's no use pretending, Jendy dear. She was never easy to live with, and now it's . . . she's . . . Quite honestly, it's making me ill. I simply can't stand this sort of thing."

"Couldn't you go away?"

"And leave the house to them?" He shuddered.

"Won't Beulah be going back to school soon? Quarantine doesn't last forever."

"There's a plan . . . I feel it's so dreadful

that I try not to believe it — of keeping Beulah here until Anabel decides . . . Well, there's no use in hinting to you, Jendy. You'll hear gossip about it soon enough."

"Gossip?"

"Everybody knows that Anabel is here because Roderick is here. Everybody. She makes no secret of it; she goes up — you must see her — to the farm every day. If she married him, I don't suppose I'd see much of her or of Beulah — but to have them so near, after so many happy years. . . ."

Tears, now, were not far away. She could do nothing but murmur phrases in which the word "patience" occurred with monotonous frequency. But his afternoon was ruined, and he took his leave and went forlornly away, his dejected stoop contrasting oddly with his tripping, springy walk. She went back to the house wondering how long Anabel gave herself to capture Roderick Harvey. — And then the sight of the Petersons' car drove Anabel from her mind.

Mrs. Peterson proved to be a short, square, solid-looking woman with an air as truculent as her husband's. Jendy, who had expected her to be thin and mild-eyed and even wild-eyed, found the picture as much out of focus as the one she had had of Beulah. But there were contrasts about Mrs. Peterson's appearance which she found interesting and which helped to allay the boredom of the visit: the hard, red face surmounted by a mop of frizzy permanent waves; the chin that jutted outward and the forehead that sloped backward; the fluffy pink blouse worn with a heavy tweed suit of the same material and almost the same cut as her husband's.

And like her husband, Mrs. Peterson appeared to have no time for niceties.

"Oldish house," she commented, having completed the preliminaries of greeting.

"Fifteen eighty-ish," said Aunt Eddie.

"My word!" The exclamation was one of commiseration. "I suppose you can't do anything about the drafts, then. Must be cold all the year round."

"Not a bit," lied Aunt Eddie. "It's those modern flimsily built houses that let in all the drafts. I wouldn't change this for anything else."

"Well, I would," said Mrs. Peterson flatly, and gave her attention to Jendy. "You staying here?"

"Yes."

"Long?"

"I hope so."

"No job?"

"Not at the moment."

"Funny. I thought all girls these days trained for something. To get away from home, mostly. They like to get up to London and look for husbands. You engaged?"

"No."

"You must be . . . how old? Twenty-two, three?"

"Four."

"Time enough, I suppose. My mother didn't believe in early marriages. Wait till you've got some sense, she said. D'you cook?"

"I can."

"Give me a place with a good kitchen. If I'd seen this one before I came down here, I wouldn't have signed the lease till they did something about it. I don't know how landlords have the nerve to ask the rents they do, and then don't do a thing to the property. — Did Mr. Peterson tell you about the child that watches us from up a tree?"

"Yes, he did."

"I'm just waiting for her," Mrs. Peterson said grimly. "I've got my eyes open."

"They're beautiful trees," said Aunt Eddie. "I'm glad Mr. Harvey isn't going to cut them down."

"He the one that's building?" Mr. Peterson

asked. "I heard something about him wanting to buy a bit of land on our side. Well, you can tell him from me that there's going to be no pacing out or measuring while I'm a tenant. Privacy is what I'm paying for, and when I've sorted out that snooping kid, privacy's what I'll have."

"How long," Aunt Eddie asked in tones of foreboding, "are you going to stay in the house?"

"We haven't decided," Mrs. Peterson said. "Long or short, as the case may be."

The visit could not be called a success. On the departure of the guests, Aunt Eddie drew a breath of relief.

"Never again," she said.

"Not even if you're still sorry for them?"

"Not even to find out whether those dreadful little curls were her own hair or somebody else's. Now go and see if that young man of Greta's has arrived. If he has, bring him in here. Without Greta."

Jendy had some difficulty in locating Wally. He had come, Greta reported. He had looked into the kitchen, and on being informed that Aunt Eddie was entertaining visitors, he had gone on a private tour of the house.

She found him at last in the gallery that

ran the whole length of the house — walking slowly down the line of family portraits, his scarlet cap pushed to the back of his head, an absorbed frown on his brow.

"Previous owners?" he asked, as Jendy came up to him.

"Yes."

"Hugh Bertrand Latimer, sixteen-forty to seventeen-oh-five. Next? Son?"

"Yes."

"Bertrand Hugh Latimer . . . father to son, father to son. Not so much alike that you'd have trouble telling them apart, are they?"

"The women of the family look alike; the men don't."

"The good old days: enough money, enough food, cheap labor and a place like this to settle down in. Was it only the eldest son that got a place in the line?"

"Yes. The other portraits — younger sons, wives and daughters — are in various parts of the house, but —"

"But this gallery's reserved for the owners?"

"Yes."

"Hugh Bertrand; Bertrand Hugh; Hugh Bertrand. Never a Willie or a Johnnie or a Joe?"

"Never."

"Why hang up the men and not their wives?"

"The men are the direct heirs — one after another, generation after generation."

"And now no more?"

"No more."

"And that upsets you?"

"It's beginning to. I didn't think much about it when I was younger. But now I can see the . . . the continuity . . ."

"Did any of them do anything — good or bad — that got 'em into the headlines?"

"I don't think so."

"Retiring types. No Dukedoms, no Earlships?"

"Some of them married titles."

"You'd think," said Wally, walking down the line once more, "that there'd be something to mark the family likeness. A nose, maybe, or fancy eyebrows. But this lot's sure a penn'orth of all-sorts. Makes it interesting, though. My Mum used to take me over picture galleries. Called it education. I didn't agree with her then, but I've done my share of picture-gazing since I met Greta. She's crazy about pictures, like my Mum. But you don't often get a chance of getting into a family exhibition like this one. Only what I

142

always think is —"

"Well?"

"When you come to think of it, everybody's family's just as long as everybody else's. If I didn't have ancestors that went back all the way, how could I be standing here now? The only difference is having it kept on record — and on all this canvas. And I suppose what you'd call tradition. But against tradition, you could put that songs-my-mother-sang-to-me stuff. That's a sort of tradition, in its way. See?"

"Yes."

"My Mum'd like to see this place. She used to pay her half crown when she was younger and could get about. Always did her best to get taken round by the Duke; said it made it come more alive. I'd like to see your aunt shoving the half crowns round; she'd sure make 'em move."

"I forgot — she's waiting to see you."

"Then let's go. But I know what she wants to see me about," he said, following Jendy to the drawing room. "She's going to call me rude names. I've been trying to figure out whether you can be an adulterer before you're married. — What happens to this place when she dies? National Trust?"

"I don't know."

"Couldn't you and your sister — the one they call Nancy, who buzzed off before the wedding — couldn't either of you keep it? You could marry millionaires and do the place up."

"There doesn't seem any chance of it at the moment."

She went into the drawing room and Wally, at her heels, pulled off his cap — and with it seemed to come a year or two of his age. Aunt Eddie, standing stiffly in the middle of the room, began to speak as soon as he entered.

"I sent for you," she said, "because I want to say something. Your business is your business — until it becomes my business. As Greta is working for me, I feel justified in taking an interest in her welfare."

"She told me you'd hit the roof and come down stunned," said Wally. "I didn't mean to —"

"I find her useful and efficient," swept on Aunt Eddie. "Not only that. I find her an exceptionally nice girl. But I gather that you have not thought it worth while marrying her, in spite of the fact that your child is to be born in less than three weeks. She —"

"Between three and four, I make it," said Wally, after a brief calculation. "Seems no

144

time at all since —"

"She suggested that you come to this house in the evenings to help with some of the heavier work, and —"

"Be a pleasure," said Wally cordially. "I'd give a lot to have the run of a house like this. Beautiful isn't the word. It —"

"Will you kindly attend to what I am saying? In my opinion, you should be ashamed to let your wi — to let Greta do any work of this kind in her condition. It's only because I felt that it would be better for her here than in that cramped little caravan of yours that I agreed. . . . Are you listening to me?"

Wally brought his gaze reluctantly from the ceiling.

"Eh?"

"Have you heard one word of what I've been saying to you?"

"Off and on. I was looking at that ceiling. Pendants at the intersections, just like the book said. Never thought I'd see 'em with my own eyes. My Mum worked for a time in one of these show houses, and that's what got me interested. Little chap, I was; nine or ten, and weedy for my age. You'd never have thought I'd develop the way I did. My Mum was a nurse. Maternity. Used to live at Tooting, but I brought her down to a cottage not so far from here — matter of a couple of hours' drive — when she retired. She —"

"This is most interesting," broke in Aunt Eddie, "but it is entirely beside the point. I am trying to tell you that —"

"I heard that bit. I didn't marry Greta. Well, I will. Just give me time, that's all."

"Time! You have had —"

"Nine months short of three weeks; quite right, quite right. But take it this way. Lately, we've been on the move from here to there and back again, and —"

"What gives people like you the right to bring illegitimate children into the world?" demanded Aunt Eddie.

Wally's gaze had begun to wander, but her passionate tone brought his eyes to rest in wonder on her face.

"You're really taking this to heart, aren't you?" he said slowly.

"I am simply trying to make you do the right thing by Greta, that's all. I consider that —"

"Well, why don't we sit down and talk comfortably?" he suggested. He pushed a chair toward her, and to Jendy's surprise, her aunt took it. "That's better. Now I can

146

sit on this window seat, so's not to defile the nice brocade, and we can sift this thing. First: you think I've —"

"I simply want you to marry her before the baby's born, that's all. Do you *want* an illegitimate child?"

"Well" — Wally looked thoughtful — "I hadn't gone into it, if you want the truth. The fact is that my own mother didn't go into it, either, and I can't say that having no Papa I could produce on demand ever made any difference to me one way or another. I got called a bastard at school once or twice — for the right reason — but people call each other bastards all the time, and it doesn't mean a thing. Maybe I got used to the idea, and —"

"Isn't that all the more reason for you to want to give your child a name?"

"Oh, he's having that, all right. He's going to be called —"

"If I see Mr. Waybridge and talk to him and get him to arrange a marriage between you and Greta, will you agree to being married?"

"Well, I've no objection — only the cost. What do they set the figure at?"

"There will be — there will have to be, at this late stage — a special license. There will also be one or two fees, which I'm prepared to pay. I —"

"That's nice of you," Wally said. "but if it doesn't come too high, I'd rather fork out for myself. I'm getting solvent, slowly-slowly. I'm earning more now — with overtime — than I ever did in an office."

"You were in an office?" Aunt Eddie asked in surprise, before she could stop herself.

"For a whole year. My own desk and a little chair that went round and round; nine to five and a room that the sun never got into, twelve by ten, dry rot in the floor boards and a view of the back end of a block of flats. I did it because my Mum was ambitious for me; she said I'd get on fast in an office. While you're getting on, you're rotting, if you want my opinion. And that weekly pay envelope gave me a frightened feeling. They say it makes you feel more secure, but it made me feel sort of trapped. And getting on, in that office, meant moving out of my cubbyhole, which was really the filing room, and being promoted to a stool in a room with four other chaps — and I couldn't have stuck that. All that kept me going was having myself to myself, even if I did have to pop out every time a bell rang. Booth, do this;

Booth, do that. If it hadn't been for my canary, I'd have packed it up before it packed me up."

"You had a canary — in an office?" Aunt Eddie asked.

"Sure thing. Hanging in the window, singing like mad. Now it's in the caravan, singing like mad. I always think that if he could talk, he'd make you laugh, because it was in my little room that the boss must have spent a lot of nights, cooking the books."

"Cooking the . . . ?"

"Faking the records. But he didn't do a good job; they got wise to him and the firm broke up."

"Broke up?"

"Well, it had to. He was the boss, and he went to jug."

"Went to . . . ?"

"Jug. The calaboose."

"The . . . ?"

"Prison. He's doing a stretch. Embezzlement."

"Your — your employer went to — to prison?"

"He sure did. Thirty thousand quid, all in all — and you know something? I didn't even get my last two weeks' pay. There I was one morning, doing this and that and twirling round in my chair every so often, for exercise, and talking to the canary — and suddenly there were the police. Not bobbies in helmets, you understand. Quiet-looking chaps, just asking innocent little questions. And after that, I was out; I was first out, because they wanted to have a look round that filing room first thing. They wouldn't even let me stop to unhook the canary's cage — so I went back that night and fetched it. And that's working in an office for you."

"Didn't you ever train for a profession?" asked Aunt Eddie.

For the first time, they heard his laugh — loud, jibing, but infectious.

"Profession? Try it without dough," he invited. "Try it when you've been brought up on a nurse's salary. My Mum did her best, but it didn't run to training fees — and I wasn't a bright boy and so I didn't win any scholarships. I only got bright later, when it was too late. When I left school, I went into the Navy — for the fresh air. I wish I'd stayed there, but then I wouldn't have met Greta. Which reminds me — we were talking about Greta."

Aunt Eddie, who had been thinking about the canary, brought herself with an effort to concentrate on the matter in hand.

"Do I understand," she asked, "that you will marry Greta if I make all the arrangements?"

"If it matters all that much, and if Greta's for it, I don't mind. I . . . That's a funny sort of Eve they've carved there, isn't it?"

"That's Jendiss Talla, for whom this house was built. If you look, you'll see her everywhere: on the stairs, on the ceilings, above the fireplaces in all the rooms." Aunt Eddie rose. "And now if you'll —"

"Built when?" Wally was wandering around the room, his hands thrust into the pockets of his jeans, his eyes everywhere. "Fifteen something, if my book knew what it was talking about."

"Fifteen eighty-three."

"And your family's lived here all that time?"

"Without a break. Now I must wish you good afternoon."

"Good afternoon." Wally's tone was absent, and he made no attempt to go. "Father to son, father to son?"

"Until now, yes. Perhaps you will kindly close the door behind you."

" 'Course. That paneling" — he walked closer to study it — "is really something, isn't it? Carved pilasters. If that's the way you pronounce them; I never said that before, only read it. And I read about inlaid woods, just like these."

Aunt Eddie looked at him curiously.

"You like houses?"

"Weren't you listening? I told you. My Mum nursed a patient in one of them, and I used to be allowed in now and then, and I remember thinking, when I got into the Great Chamber, that I'd strayed out of doors. I didn't know that anything barring a cathedral could be that big. But freezing, just like this room. You couldn't call it comfortable living exactly, could you?"

"It depends," said Aunt Eddie. "If you want to live with space and beauty and history all round you, yes. If you want to lie about in a heated house staring at your own television and listening to other people's, with wall-to-wall carpeting and rooms like boxes and nothing to distinguish your home from half a million others. . . ."

"I see what you mean," Wally said. "But living this way, you have to be hardy."

"Jendiss Talla had twelve children and they all lived to a good old age," said Aunt Eddie. "Successive generations of Latimers have —"

152

"How many altogether? Generations, I mean."

"Thirteen."

"Thirteen," repeated Wally wonderingly. "Thirteen lots of hardy Latimers, all privileged to look at that lovely ceiling. Is that Jendiss Talla up there too?"

"It is. This house was built by Hugh Bertrand Latimer — for her."

"He must have liked having her around. Over the door, too."

"Everywhere. I told you. If you're interested," said Aunt Eddie, to her own surprise, "why don't you look round the house with my niece?"

"Thanks. I've looked round a good bit on my own," he told her. "Pity so much of it's shut up. I bet it's taken a packet to keep it standing up and in decent repair."

"Yes, it has."

"Well . . . suppose I'd better go," he said reluctantly. "Did you say I could have a job here in the evenings?"

"If you want it."

He nodded, put on his cap, went out and closed the door, and then opened it and put his head around it.

"Forgot to say thank you," he said. "About the way you're getting your teeth into this business of getting Greta and me married. My Mum'll be glad, too; she's been on to me about it."

The door closed once more, and Aunt Eddie stood staring at it. Jendy had the idea that she had forgotten she was not alone in the room.

"Curious young man," she murmured.

"Do you like him?" Jendy asked.

"No, I don't. He's impertinent and he takes far too much for granted — but he's interesting."

And he's the first person, said Jendy, but not aloud, who's ever succeeded in holding the stage when you've been on it. Or who ever talked you down. Or who ever managed to take the conversation out of your hands into his own.

An interesting young man indeed, she thought.

CHAPTER 6

"An' I went down a mine, and I dug," said Beulah. "In Wales."

"I went digging for gold in Alaska once," said Wally, without pausing in his work of dragging out a particularly tenacious piece of undergrowth. "I found some, too."

Jendy was watching from a comfortable seat on a tree stump. Behind him stood Beulah, feet apart, hands thrust into the pockets of her mackintosh, on her face an expression compounded equally of hate and hopelessness. Her lies had become phenomenal — but they could not match Wally's. She was outclassed, and knew it; he could fill in, could shape, could color, could trip her up on details. He had exposed her geographically, biologically, zoologically. And anatomically, for in this sphere he could turn her most artistic efforts. Worse, he could turn her stomach.

"— and the walls all fell in," Jendy heard her saying, "an' I couldn't get out. My head was all bashed, and —"

"If it'd been really bashed," said Wally, "you'd have been a goner. You'd have had your brains bashed out, and that would've meant that they . . . What's the matter? Got to go?"

"It's time for my lunch."

"Oh well. But it's funny how if you get a really hard bash, all your brains sort of . . . Oh, ta-ta."

"Why do you do it?" Jendy asked him, as Beulah went hastily away.

"Why? To get rid of her. And to teach her, too. She all but turned my insides at first, with her juicy bits."

"It seems almost a shame to beat her at her own game."

"In a way it is, because it's too easy. But if I didn't get her to skedaddle, she'd bring a stool and camp just behind me, trying to get my goat. — Was her mother like that when she was young?"

"No. She was thin, for one thing — thin and dark. Not pretty. In fact, rather ugly, but as she grew older, she became more and more attractive; still not in the least pretty, but with looks of a kind that — what the French call —"

"I know; I've been to school. Jolly laid. Yes, I can see that. And sexy, too. You can see why all those men buzzed round, marrying her — even though they knew they'd have to swallow the kid — that kid. Pity one of her stepfathers didn't apply a bit of correction in the right place. Not that she isn't well padded. Isn't Nature wonderful? She provides protection just where it's needed."

Jendy did not answer. It was too good a day to be discussing Beulah. The sun was warm — too warm. This was weather that they should have in the summer, and probably wouldn't. The grass was dry and the clearing on which Wally was working smelled of wood and warm earth. From where she sat, she could see cows moving lazily across the fields below; smoke was rising from the kitchen chimney of the farmhouse and dispersing slowly in the light breeze. Workmen's voices floated down from the site; trucks tipped their loads with a scrunching, scrambling noise and then drove away. Allen appeared in the distance for a moment before disappearing into the feed store. A woman's voice — Anabel's —

answered a man's — Roderick's. They were up there.

But she had been up there with Roderick until she had seen Anabel arriving at the farm — and then she had strolled down to talk to Wally. It was a new game, and she was enjoying it.

Anabel had begun it. Coming daily to the farm, she had seen, had sometimes passed close to, Jendy. On the first occasion, when Jendy had been going out of the gate as Anabel came in, she had stopped, expecting the other woman at least to utter a word or two of greeting. But Anabel had swept on, unseeing, her gaze directed toward the building site where she knew Roderick would be, and the action had said more plainly than any words could have done that essentials were essentials — and wasting time with Jendy, or with Allen, was at this moment clearly nonessential. First things first, with the courtesies following a very long way behind.

But it was Allen who issued invitations to meals — to Jendy. It was Allen with whom Roderick liked to spend the hour before dinner. It was in Allen's house that drinks were dispensed, plans for the details of the house discussed, family matters gone into.

Anabel could have Roderick — when he was at her disposal. But there were times when he was not. And at those times, Anabel was shut out — and Jendy admitted. She was with Allen most of the day; she was with Wally for part of the day — but she knew that she was spending far more time in Roderick's company than she would have believed possible when she first came back to Tallahouse. And she was spending far more time in Roderick's company than Anabel liked.

And Roderick, she mused, was without doubt good company. With Allen, she was at ease; sometimes they scarcely spoke, content to enjoy long, comfortable silences, content in one another's society. With Roderick, she had to be alert. His views were clearer-cut and more clearly expressed than Allen's. Allen felt his way through problems; Roderick cut his way through them. He was still difficult to read, but she found it stimulating to try and find out what lay behind his dark eyes — or his enigmatic remarks.

The patch of sun moved, and Jendy followed it, leaned against a tree trunk and realized that nothing had turned out as she had expected. She had come to Tallahouse wondering whether she could get on with Aunt Eddie — and had discovered in her an entertaining and affectionate companion. She had imagined that Nancy's presence would hang like a cloud over the farm, slowly dispersing as time healed Allen's wounds. Instead, they spoke of her frequently and naturally, and there was no cloud. No visible cloud. She had learned, if not to understand, then how to manage Roderick; manage was not the word she wanted, but it would serve to explain their present pleasant relations.

Allen and Roderick. Wally and Greta. Aunt Eddie. And sun and beauty and peace. And, she realized with deep thankfulness, happiness of a kind she had not dreamed of. For she was happy. She knew that at the bottom of her mind, Nancy and Nancy's absence lay heavily — but this was an interval of happiness; a time for setting aside problems and enjoying the present.

She was happy — and to give a balance, there was Anabel, and Beulah. She was happy, and she could put aside, for the moment, perplexing questions: how much Allen was feeling; why Roderick spent so much time with her. He might want Anabel to feel — as she herself wanted her to feel — that she was not having things all her own way. Whatever the reason, he sought her out frequently — and Anabel couldn't like it.

Wally also seemed to dislike it.

"Now we're alone, you and me," he said, suspending work and turning to look at her, "how about listening to some good advice?"

"I'm listening," she said.

"Well, watch your step. See what I mean?"

"No. Explain."

"You can't always explain things you feel. And sometimes there's nothing to say — like when you see someone trotting along, bound for the cliff edge and not seeming to know it. All you can do then is holler. I'm hollering. Can you hear me?"

"I hear you. What's over the cliff edge?"

"Trouble. Trouble with Mrs. Thrice-wed. She doesn't waste time looking at me, but when she's walking round wondering where her boy friend's got to, I can look at her — and I don't like what I see. And I'm serious. It isn't my business, but then neither is it your aunt's business to get me married — but that's what she's doing, and one way I can pay it back is to tell you that you're not really cut out for what you're trying to do."

"What am I trying to do?"

"Get Anabel Thrice-wed's goat. You can stop trying. You've got it, so now give it back and stick to Mr. Allen Harvey and let the other one alone."

"Look, Wally" — Jendy had risen and was standing facing him — "this isn't really —"

"I know, I know, I know. Down, dog! Well, you just let me yap on for a bit while I tell you that I may seem to be slaphappy in some ways, but I know people. Brought up the way I've been, you get to know all sorts. And I'm telling you that this Anabel Thrice-wed is dynamite — see? You wait a bit, and she blows up. And if you're hanging around when she blows up, you're liable to get hurt. And nobody seems to be telling you — which is why I am. I thought Harvey the Elder might have tipped you off, but all he sees is that little brother and little-sister-of-Nancy are hitting it off better than he ever thought they would. They don't snarl at each other any more — ain't that fine? Goody-goody; one big, happy family. But he should've told you what I'm telling you: lay off this Anabel. Why Harvey the younger lets you do it, I can't think; all I can say is that he must have reasons of his own, and I don't care to state what they are. All I'm worried about, as at this moment, is you. You're the niece of someone who's going out

162

of her way to do something for me — more important, something for Greta — and I can't go on mauling this jungle until I've told you not to get between Harvey the younger and the lady who's after him. She won't get him. He's got all his buttons done up, and for him, as the Bible would put it, I hath no fear. He's all right. He's all there and more so. But you're . . . you're. . . ."

"I'm . . . ?"

"Well, you're angry, for one thing, but that's only to be expected. But you're . . . if you wait, I'll hit on the word I want. You're . . . tender. No. Inexperienced? I hope not. I've got it: you're vulnerable. That's it. I didn't know I knew a word that long, but it fits. You're vulnerable. You're open to hurt, open to being hurt, open to being badly hurt. That Anabel's in one class, and you're in another. So put away your little pea-shooter and stick to games with rules. You know about David and Goliath? Well, what really happened was that little David took a shot, and it hit old Goliath all right, but all it did was give him a slight clunk on the head — so what does he do? After making sure it was no bumblebee, but that brash kid with his catapult, he goes over and picks up David, and . . . This is the bit where Beulah has to go home to lunch. Certificate X. But that's what happens in real life to the Davids, and that's you. So lay off, and next time Harvey Junior wants your company for reasons I won't go into, you just say: Push off. Buzz off. Back to base. See?"

There was a long silence. They looked at one another: the girl in a lightweight coat, bareheaded, feet in low-heeled country shoes; the young man in jeans, with his scarlet cap and under it an expression of unwonted seriousness on his clear-skinned, handsome face.

"See?" he asked again. "Be as angry as you want to, but take my advice and don't make this Anabel angry. She's dangerous. What you're doing's dangerous."

And exactly how dangerous it was, Jendy learned — a little — that afternoon, when she met Anabel on the slope that led up to the building site.

This time, there was no brushing past. Anabel came to a halt, her greenish, contemptuous eyes on Jendy.

"Oh, hello," she said. "I've seen you around. Staying long?"

"I think so."

"Holding Aunt Eddie's hand? She must

have taken a knock: favorite godson and favorite niece. I can't say I blame Nancy; Allen's not my idea of a stimulant. But I forgot — perhaps you're holding his hand too? — How's Nancy?"

"Very well, thank you."

"How's she enjoying Seville?"

There was, Jendy noted with inexplicable panic welling up in her, the same tone in Anabel's voice as there had been in Roderick's when she had told him that Nancy was in Seville.

"I haven't heard from her," she said, "since —"

"— she got there? Perhaps you won't. Perhaps she's too busy. Perhaps . . ."

Her voice trailed way in a gurgle of amusement. The gurgle became a peal, and then another, and another. Head back, shoulders shaking, Anabel had given way to helpless laughter. But there was no mirth in the sound. There was a terrifying triumph. It was laughter in which there were jeering, contemptuous notes.

Jendy waited. She wanted to move away, but something held her to the spot. When the devil-laughter had subsided, she could ask. . . .

But Anabel spoke first, still laughing, her

mocking eyes on the other woman.

"It's so terribly, terribly funny," she said. "It was the funniest thing I'd heard for years. Nancy . . . at Seville!"

The laughter broke out again — and this time it was not Jendy who waited for it to stop. Roderick's voice put a cold question.

"What's funny, Anabel?"

Anabel swung around, speaking in a high, excited voice.

"Everything. Nancy at Seville — and Jendy obviously thinking she's gone there for the Feria! Or something. Isn't it too funny for words?"

"Not as funny as all that," Roderick said. "Now will you stop annoying Jendy, and go home?"

"If you'll come too," said Anabel, and laughed again.

He hesitated. Then:

"All right; I'll go," he said.

"It's a deal," said Anabel. "But first let me tell Jendy what —"

"Come on," he said, and something in his voice brought her eyes to his face. Whatever she saw there made her shrug and smile; then without a word to Jendy, she took his hand and led him down the hill toward his car.

And Jendy stood where she was and let hate flood over her — hate for them both. Hate for Anabel. Hate for Roderick Harvey. Misery and panic fought within her — and then the panic subsided. Anabel had tried to frighten her. There was nothing to be frightened of. But Roderick . . . he had allowed her to commit herself to a pledge of friendship. She had been in his company, enjoyed his company — more fantastic still, spent even more time with him, lately, than she had with Allen.

And he was down there, going out of sight — with Anabel Druce. And Anabel was still laughing. . . .

Laughter — because Nancy was at Seville. Laughter — because Nancy had left Madrid and gone to Seville and was staying with Carlos and Milagros Navarrete. . . .

The sun was still shining, but the brightness seemed to have gone out of the day. She went slowly down to the white gates, and for the first time walked out of them without going to say a word to Allen.

She walked slowly homeward, her mind so far from her surroundings that when Wally's car pulled up in front of her, she had some difficulty in recognizing it. Then Wally leaned out and addressed her.

"How about coming into the village with us?" he asked.

She made an effort to speak naturally.

"No work this afternoon?" she asked.

"Half day. I gave myself one and your aunt gave Greta one. Coming?"

She hesitated, and Wally's eyes rested on her face.

"Everything all right?" he asked.

"Quite all right," she answered evenly. "I just haven't got any shopping to do, that's all."

"Then come for the drive," he said.

He got down, and she allowed him to help her to a seat beside Greta.

"Mind your clothes on the door," he warned. "The car's dirty."

"Because it is his job to clean it," said Greta. "The caravan is clean because it is my job."

"Take a look at the shopping list." Wally handed it to her and started the car once more. "Sugar, salt, olive oil, cornflakes and cheese. Can you think of anything else?"

"Tea?" suggested Jendy.

"Your aunt gave us a supply. Great woman, your aunt. I don't know why I didn't fall in love with her at first sight. Does she unite in holy matrimony all the livers-in-sin she happens to come across?"

"Not all," said Jendy. "She'd like to. She thinks that the other way, the men get the best of it."

"And that makes her mad?"

"Yes."

Some of the misery was draining out of her. There was something under Wally's light manner that seemed to reach out and reassure her. He had warned her. He had called her vulnerable — and the meeting with Anabel had proved him right. She had no weapon with which to counter Anabel's spite. Her only hope had lain in not arousing her antagonism — but she had thought herself capable of matching herself against her.

She looked out through Wally's fly-pitted windscreen and wondered exactly what she had been trying to prove to Anabel. Something . . . something she did not care to analyze. Not yet. Not now.

"She gets mad," Wally was saying, "what for? Because the women give all and the men take all, or something?"

"Yes."

"She likes them to pay for their fun?"

"She likes them to pay for their privileges."

"I get that," Wally said. "But about this marrying me off . . . Did you know that she's going to have a sort of afterwedding do at Tallahouse?"

"Yes. She told me."

"Well, fixing things at the church is one thing — but having a party at the house afterward is what my Mum calls sewing on the frills. What'll the village make of it?"

"The village," Jendy said, "will put it down as just one more example of the eccentricity of the Latimers. I can't answer for the Latimer women who came before Aunt Eddie, but I know that ever since I've lived here, she has done exactly as she wanted to, without any regard for what the village would think."

"Things like — ?"

"Like adopting every Fair that came to Oxterley, and arranging a temporary launderette service for the wives — and baths for the children. Like making Mr. Waybridge hold open-air services for the cycling club before they took off on Sundays. Like building a hall and buying a record player so that the teenagers could dance instead of hanging about. Like getting a school bus put on for the very small ones. It all sounds easy — but it wasn't. It wasn't as though there was a committee of women to arrange it, as there might have been if there'd been more big houses round here. Aunt Eddie did it alone. At least, she started off alone, and ended by sweeping the village along with her."

"You mean there aren't any other local do-gooders?"

"None. The Druces — the old Druces, Anabel's mother and father — hid behind imaginary ailments. The tenants of Ravenscroft were never here for long, so you couldn't expect them to be interested in local affairs. The Harveys were genuinely tied up with farm work. So Aunt Eddie does things on her own."

"Is it true that the village used to be a smuggler's headquarters?" Greta asked.

"Quite true. You won't find one of those old cottages without its hiding place. Oxterley was nicely placed for smugglers — just three miles from a nice, secluded cove, and not too easy to get at in those days — from the land side."

"Did any of the Latimer gents have a hand in it?" Wally asked.

"The Latimer gents," said Jendy, "always had a hand in everything — but it wasn't always the same hand. Sometimes it was the right and sometimes it was the left. Hugh Bertrand helped the smugglers, but Bertrand Hugh chased them. One Latimer might be all for witch-hunting, but the next one would be dead against it."

"One yelled for Charles and the other rooted for Cromwell," went on Wally. "I get it. What did the last Latimer go for? Not women, by the sound of it. Was he Hugh Bertrand, or Bertrand Hugh?"

"Bertrand Hugh."

"Well, I agree with your aunt," Wally said. "He didn't done his dooty. He should've left twelve kids up there at Tallahouse, like the first one did. Twelve kids could've done a lot to the place. He could've made the first one a carpenter, the next a plumber — and so on. These days, you've got to do-it-yourself, and you can't start training kids too soon. I couldn't get my Mum to see that, though. Laboring, she called it. She didn't want me to labor . . . only in an office. These ambitious women — you can't hold 'em. — Well, here we are."

He pulled up at the grocer's and looked at Jendy.

"How about coming in with us?" he asked. "You'd be a help. The grocer's waiting to be paid for the last lot of stuff I got off him when we drove in. You'll be able to explain to him that in my life, the pay follows the job — and tomorrow's pay day."

"Are you," Jendy inquired, "asking me to be responsible for your bills?"

"That's the idea." He was out of the car, helping her and Greta out. "You trust me and the grocer'll trust you. How about it?"

She hesitated, but not for long. An unpaid bill or two, she thought, looking at the smiling young pair, was small payment for enjoying their freshness and charm. It might be unsound logic — but she liked them both. In gay but shabby attire, without anything more than the prospect of a few weeks' wages, with a baby soon to be provided for, Wally leaned against the grocer's counter with an air of needing nothing more in the world than he had already, explaining airily to the grocer that Miss Marsh would take care of everything.

"You're a trusting chap," he said gratefully, when the grocer had expressed his willingness to take Jendy's word. "If we leave here without paying, we'll leave our blessings — won't we, Greta? No, not that cheese, old chap. I'd rather have the wormy kind; more body. That's it; that'll do fine."

He stuffed his purchases into a string bag

and shepherded his two companions outside.

"That's all for us. How about you?" he asked Jendy. "Oh — you said you didn't need anything. That makes three of us with all we want in the world — nice thought, no?"

Jendy looked at him.

"Oughtn't you . . ."

She paused, and Wally prompted her.

"— to — ?"

"Well, there are some things, aren't there, that you'll need, or Greta'll need," she said, and plunged on before prudence could halt her. "I mean things for the baby. A cot and a — Perhaps I could help. Unless you've got all the baby's things."

"Why would we have the baby's things?" he asked in surprise. "He won't be here for a couple of weeks."

"But he might —"

"— jump the gun? If he does, I'll pop out while Greta's producing him, and nip back with the necessary. Not that I'll need to. You'd be surprised how nervous people get when they think you haven't provided for the future. I like that bit about the lilies of the field being arrayed like Solomon. You've just shown why: They reap not, neither do they sow, but that drives the neighbors clean

174

crazy with anxiety, and so they get together and hurry along with some of Solomon's clothes, and array the lily. It can't miss. Weren't you — admit it — just going to rush off and buy underpants for the baby?"

"I was."

"And I stopped you. But when I don't know that people are going to provide for Greta and me and the baby, I can't stop them, can I?"

"Would you?" Jendy asked.

"It depends. Your aunt, for instance; she's whipping up steam about what she calls a layette. Isn't it going to make her as happy as Christmas, taking Greta out and buying one?"

"Yes," agreed Jendy. "It is."

"Then why stop her? We pay it back in other ways — I think. I hope. And now hop in and I'll run you back to Tallahouse and your kind aunt."

"I'll take her back," came Roderick's voice behind them.

"Ah, here's my boss." Wally turned and surveyed him with leisurely coolness. "Miss Marsh," he told him, "has just been explaining to the grocer that I'm a chap he can give credit to."

"Then she's very silly," said Roderick.

"Pity you weren't here in time to stop her," said Wally. "You mean you wouldn't have done the same?"

"I would not, and you know it," said Roderick. "Anybody who stands security for somebody they know nothing about is asking for trouble. Why didn't you come to me and ask for an advance on your pay?"

"Risky," explained Wally. "Some people take you on trust, like Miss Marsh here; other people don't and won't, like you. What I can't understand is why the boss can always ask for a good character, while the fellows like me have to take the boss on trust. Look at my last one. Did I tell you he got roped in for embezzlement?"

"No, you didn't," said Roderick.

"Well, that's what happened. I was two weeks' pay out of pocket, and he'd swindled the public to the tune of thirty thousand quid. That's bosses for you. With that experience behind me, I ought to have seen to it that you paid me in advance. — Did you say you wanted to take Miss Marsh home?"

"No. I said I was going to take Miss Marsh home."

"Well, well, well." Wally grinned engagingly. He was about a head shorter than

Roderick, but his slender, lithe figure seemed to give him extra height. "Let's hear what Miss Marsh has to say about it."

Roderick was not smiling, but his eyes, resting on the younger man, held something between amusement and speculation. Jendy thought he had a wary air, as though he was waiting for Wally to go too far.

"I'll go with Mr. Harvey," she said.

She would go with him — and she would make him tell her exactly why Anabel Druce had laughed. She would find out what lay behind his brief description of the Navarretes. She took a step toward him, only to find Wally's hand on her arm.

"Half a minute," he said. "I'm your aunt's handyman and I have to look after you."

Roderick laughed.

"All you have to look after," he said, "is your own business. Run away and don't keep Greta standing in the road."

"I was only going to tell Miss Marsh a short story — the one about the good brother and the bad brother," Wally said casually. "Won't take a minute."

Roderick, who had turned toward his car, looked back.

"What happened in the end?" he asked.

"Well, someone came along," said Wally,

177

"and warned the princess about the smooth guy who was being taken for a ride by Mrs. Thrice-wed. So she — hey! That's not the end!"

"Some other time," called Roderick, leading Jendy across the narrow little street.

He was smiling as he settled her into his car.

"One day," he said, "that young fellow'll take one step too many and walk over the edge."

"I like him," Jendy said.

"So do I. But liking's nothing to do with it. Allen thinks he's shady."

She was so astounded that he had got in beside her and driven some distance before she could bring out an incredulous echo.

"*Shady!* Wally?"

"Yes." He glanced at her. "Why not?"

"Why not? Why . . . because he's . . . he's —"

"— good-looking, with what's called an open countenance?"

"Because he's —"

"— got winning ways?"

"What," she fell back on asking, "has Allen got against him?"

"Little things. Disquieting things all the same. Small discrepancies in the information he hands out."

"Such as?"

"About his parents, mostly. What did he tell you about his mother?"

"He told Aunt Eddie that she used to be a nurse and . . . and she worked in a house rather like Tallahouse when he was about nine or ten."

"Quite. That's what he told me — casually, whenever I dropped down to see how he was getting on with the job. But he told Allen she'd died when he was born."

"What else?" Jendy asked after a pause.

"He told me his father took to the bottle and was supported by his mother until he died — when Wally was about three. He told Allen that his father had made himself scarce before he was born and had never shown up since. Small things, as I said — but Allen thinks they count."

"I . . . I can't believe there's anything wrong with him," she said slowly. "I just can't."

"I can."

"Why?"

"Because he goes prowling at night."

"He . . . he *what?*"

"Goes prowling round the place after dark. I caught him at it quite by chance when I'd walked up to the site to see what the view looked like by moonlight. It looked pretty good — so good that I must have stood there for some time without moving, just looking at it. Then I heard something — and thought it was a small animal of some kind. But it wasn't. It was a man's figure creeping with the utmost caution down the slope toward the farmhouse. He was in shadow — and so was I. But I had an advantage: I knew he was there, but he didn't know that I was there. So I stood where I was — and to my amazement saw that it was Wally."

"He was . . ."

"Prowling. I watched him as he got down to the level of the house; I was certain he'd been watching it, waiting for the lights to go out before trying to break in — if that's what he was going to do. But when he went past, he didn't even slow down. He ducked and took it carefully, keeping in cover, but he went straight past and on to the caravan. What he was doing up at the site, I don't know — but I'll find out."

There was silence. A weight of depression settled on her. Wally. . . .

"What did Allen say when you told him?" she asked at last.

"I didn't tell him."

"But he's got to know!"

"Not necessarily. He's got his suspicions, and that puts him on his guard. I've got more than suspicions — but if I tell Allen, he'll have him thrown off the place, and if he gets rid of him, I'll never find out what he's after. Asking him would be no use; can you see Wally parting with any information he wanted to keep to himself? I'd get lots of answers — but not the right one. So I'm on the lookout. I've moved to one of the rooms that overlook the site, and I've got a good view of anybody going up or coming down. He's been out every night, just prowling — but so far, nothing more. So I'm waiting."

Once more there was silence — and then she realized that in the shock caused by hearing of Wally's inexplicable actions, she had not realized that the car was not going toward Tallahouse.

"This isn't the way home," she said.

"No. You looked as though you needed a drive."

"Well, I don't. I'd like to go home."

"We're going home — the long way round."

"In that case, you'll have time to tell me," she said, "what Anabel found so amusing about the fact that Nancy was in Seville."

"Is in Seville?"

"Is or was. Why was she laughing?"

"The things that amuse Anabel aren't as a rule the things that amuse people like you."

"I dare say not. But why was she laughing? It was because she knew, and you know, something about the Navarretes that you won't tell me."

"I told you they were what you call not-nice. I even told you why."

"Why did she laugh?"

"With a little effort, you can work it out for yourself. She laughed because she's always known that people like the Navarretes weren't Nancy's sort of people. They were her sort. My sort. One of the things that Anabel has always had against you both, as you know, is the fact that you bypassed every one of the men she brought down to Gannets. You climbed up — she thinks — on a couple of pedestals, and from there, looked down in all senses on her and on her friends. She didn't like that. Calling you too pure to live, or calling you prudish or out of date or narrow-minded or strait-laced gave her a certain amount of satisfaction, but not enough; you were still sitting up there. So when she realizes that one of you has climbed down; that Nancy doesn't only know the

Navarretes but is actually living in their house, she thinks it's funny. Nancy off what Anabel calls her high horse — at last. Nancy in Anabel's own set — at last. So she laughs."

"There's something more. The first time I mentioned —"

"Did you ever know a time when Anabel wasn't only too anxious to broadcast unpleasant truths?"

"No."

"Then — if you're sure there's something more, why don't you ask her what it is? Ask her. If she knew anything about Nancy that she thought would hurt you, do you think for a moment she'd keep it to herself?"

"No."

So much, at least, she could be certain of it. If Anabel had a weapon, she would use it.

Some of the strain, the pain drained out of her. Roderick glanced at her, but he said no more until they reached Tallahouse. Then he stopped the car and put a hand on hers for a moment.

"Can't you stop worrying about Nancy?"

"No."

"Isn't it time you made yourself?"

"I suppose so. But you weren't with her for those last three days before she went back to Spain — and I was. There was something . . . something about her. . . ."

"What sort of something?" His voice was gentle.

"I don't know. All I know is that instead of accepting the idea that she's gone, I have a feeling — a feeling that's growing stronger and stronger — that . . . that . . ."

"That?"

"That Allen let her go too soon. Without a fight. Without keeping her until he'd had time, given himself time to think. It was all over too suddenly. She told him, and he accepted it, and he went with her to Tallahouse and she packed — and she went away. It was . . . it was too quick. She didn't have time. . . ."

"Can't you count? Eighteen from twenty-seven —"

"— makes a lot of years, but some people take more time than others to . . . to know what they really want. Nancy did. Nancy does. Allen shouldn't have let her go back — not so quickly. And he knows it."

"He knows what?"

"That he let go too soon."

"Let her go?"

"No. Just let go. She'd come to a crossroad, and I think now that we just let

184

her walk away. Nobody . . . Well, yes; I did — but I wasn't the one who should have, who could have given her just one last chance to . . . to think. I'm not explaining it very well, but nobody — nobody in the world knows Nancy as well as I do. Not Allen. Not Aunt Eddie. So when I say the word Seville and you dart away as though it had stung you; when I mention Seville and get nothing from you but evasions; when Anabel laughs like a maniac at the thought of Nancy's being in Seville . . . then I worry."

"I can —"

"And I'll tell you something that you oughtn't to need telling — and that is that Allen's worrying."

"How do you know?"

"Because he talks of Nancy more and more, but in a quite different way. When I came home, he mentioned her almost casually, as though he didn't want to wipe out her memory from the farm. Now . . . it isn't the same. He brings up her name again and again, and then . . . goes into a sort of uneasy dream. The shock's over; she's gone — and he feels he could have, and should have, handled it another way."

"You think it would have made any difference?"

185

"Perhaps not. I don't know. But it would have given her just that feeling that he wanted more from her than the mere statement that she couldn't live his life. If he'd driven her to the point of giving real reasons, maybe she would have found that the reasons weren't so compelling after all. So don't tell me to stop worrying, because that's why I can't."

"If she's all right, she's all right," he pointed out. "If she isn't, there's nothing you can do about it. Right or wrong, she's got to lead her own life — and you've got to lead yours. Try to put her out of your mind — for the moment. Try to forget her — for the moment. Will you?"

She looked at him for some time, and for once he could not tell what she was thinking. Her question startled him.

"Why didn't you marry Milagros?"

His eyebrows went up.

"Marry? It didn't even get as far as an engagement in the real sense." He smiled. "It was what you'd call an affair. I was lucky to get away with my tail feathers."

She would have liked to ask him whether his tail feathers were not in more danger from Anabel than they had ever been from Milagros; instead, she merely asked him if

186

he would come into the house.

"And have your aunt abusing me? No, thanks."

"Well, then — thank you for bringing me home."

"A symbolic drive," he said. "You'll always come home by the long route."

"I don't understand."

He laughed.

"One day, I'll explain. And in the meantime, don't say anything to Allen about the prowling. You won't find it difficult."

"Why not?"

"Because you're an adept at keeping secrets from Allen."

He was gone before she could think of any reply. She stood staring after the car and then walked slowly into the house, to find Aunt Eddie waiting for her.

"Wasn't that Roderick Harvey's car?"

"Yes."

"I thought so. He drives about in that luxurious affair while Allen plods about in a station wagon."

"Roderick's not a farmer."

"More shame to him. You're looking tired. Why?"

Jendy hesitated. She wanted to say that she was not tired; that she was worried and depressed — depressed because Wally was under suspicion of being a liar, a thief — or worse. But something in her was still struggling strongly against the suspicions that Roderick had voiced.

There were other things. Wally had become almost part of the household. Aunt Eddie had met in him somebody who, for the first time in her life, she could not catalogue, could not pigeonhole. And could not browbeat. He snatched off his cap deferentially at her approach and appeared to listen carefully to all she had to say, but she was aware that she had only half his attention — and that he had none of the respect for age which she looked for in the young. He regarded her, it was plain, as a benevolent old crank, and he treated her with a mixture of indulgence and firmness. His thanks for the efforts she had made on his behalf came less from the brief acknowledgments he voiced than from the steady evenings of work he did in the house. He was a magnificent handyman. Broken locks, cracked windowpanes, loose balustrades, defective plugs, neglected tools or broken-down apparatus — he found them all without being asked, mended them and put them away again without bothering to inform anybody that they were sound once more.

Wally . . . a liar? A cheat? A thief?

She heard her aunt speaking.

"What in the world is worrying you?"

"Wally."

"What about Wally?"

"Roderick's just been telling me that he and Allen think he's . . . not what he seems to be. They think he's . . . shady."

"Oh, really?" Aunt Eddie's voice grated with contempt. "They think he's shady. And they have, of course, plenty of proof of this shadiness?"

"No." Jendy frowned. "At least, they —"

"Men's intuition?"

"No. It's nothing definite, but they —"

"— just feel. But they feel without being able to prove anything?"

"There's no proof yet, but they —"

"Well, you can listen to me. Anybody can throw out hints or harbor suspicions — but you can tell Roderick and Allen Harvey that until they can come to me with substantial proof to hold up any of these allegations they're making, I shall continue to have every confidence in Wally. You can also tell anybody who's interested that I've lived a good many years, and I haven't lived without using my eyes — and my judgment. I know without being helped when I can trust somebody and when I can't. If your uncle Bertrand had trusted my judgment more, he would have been a great deal better off in every way. I like the Harveys. That is, I liked the old people and I'm fond of Allen — but as a family, they always had this tendency to pay too much attention to gossip. I'd be glad if you didn't air their suspicions, or your own, where I can hear them."

"I haven't any suspicions."

"I'm glad to hear it. Neither have I."

Jendy looked at her, willing, happy to be reassured. Her sentiments were absolutely those of her aunt. Against suspicions, she could only offer this feeling of utter confidence in Wally.

"You really think he's . . . all right?" she asked.

Aunt Eddie squared her shoulders.

"Consider," she said. "Would I — think carefully — would I take in a young man, encourage him to take an interest in this house, employ him, arrange to marry him to a decent young girl if I didn't know for certain that he was absolutely all right? Now, would I? Most certainly I would not!"

And with this unanswerable logic, Jendy was well content.

CHAPTER 7

Mr. Peterson was doing his best to find somebody who would accept responsibility for Beulah, but he was getting little satisfaction. He called upon Anabel, who was reported to have sent him away with his tail between his legs. He had waylaid Milford, but Milford's tail was always between his legs, and nothing had come of the interview but protestations that he had no responsibility for and no control over his niece.

A visit to Aunt Eddie produced very little more, but she had a little practical advice to offer.

"Buy a hose," she said. "A couple of jets of cold water never hurt anybody. Buy a hose, and once she knows you're prepared to use it, you won't have any more trouble."

"I don't have as much trouble as I did," he acknowledged. "That chap who's working on the site, clearing the ground — I'm told he keeps her on the ground while he's on the spot. It's when he goes off for his meals that she does her climbing, and that's what I'm going to put a stop to. If she'd been a man, or even a boy, I could've dealt with her. But I might just as well have taken a house and garden without a tree or a wall or a hedge round it, for all the privacy we get."

He went at last to put the matter before Allen. Allen, after listening to the opening sentences, sent a man to find and fetch Beulah.

She came marching through the yard, defiance in every step, and halted before Allen.

"Mr. Peterson's been telling me that you still climb trees and look into his garden. I thought Wally told you not to do it."

"I don't — when he's there. Why shouldn't I? You've always let me climb trees before. I don't hurt anybody."

"If you want to climb trees in your uncle's garden, you can," said Allen. "But if you're seen up those trees overlooking Mr. Peterson's garden just once more, you'll stay off this farm for good. Do you understand?"

"Yes. But it isn't fair. I was here before the Petersons came, and I've been climbing up —"

"That's all," said Allen.

"Well, I think you're jolly mean."

"I think you're jolly mean, too. Anybody who spies on other people is jolly mean. And if you get any jolly meaner, you'll be off this place so fast, you won't know how you got home. Now go away and watch your step. I'm getting tired of complaints about you. Why can't you help people — give a hand here and there about the place — instead of just making a nuisance of yourself?"

She went sulkily away, and Mr. Peterson looked after her.

"Sweet specimen," he commented. "Why d'you let her hang about the place?"

"Because if she didn't, what would she do?"

"Stay at home, where she belongs."

"In a half-acre of garden, with a mother who's totally uninterested in her, and an uncle who wishes she were somewhere else?"

"That's her problem, not yours. A kid like that ought to be under someone's eye; she wants watching. You shouldn't give her the run of a place like this; God only knows what she'll get up to."

"She's a nuisance, but at least I feel I'm giving her a bit of healthy freedom."

"She's had too much freedom by a long chalk. What she needs is a couple of minutes a day across someone's knee, getting her seat warmed. I'd like to apply; be a pleasure."

"I don't think she'll annoy you any more."

"Well, that's where we don't agree — but let's wait and see. I'll only tell you this, Harvey: if I see her again, I'll take steps. I'm warning you."

"Why warn me? Why not warn her mother?"

"Because you've decided to go on letting her come here, that's why. If you don't order her off the farm, as you should do, you can't blame me for taking matters into my own hands."

"She's only eight years old. I know nobody wants to be spied on, but what harm does she really do?"

"She watches my wife, and she goes round telling the village people she's mad — which she isn't, not by a long way. Why d'you think I took a place like that if I hadn't been certain there were plenty of thick hedges round it?"

Allen looked surprised.

"Did you come down before you took the place? I understood —"

"— that I took it unseen? Well, I didn't.

My father rented it when he came home from the East once — forty years ago and more. He brought my brother and myself here, and I remembered the place and decided it was just what I wanted. And so it would have been if that young devil hadn't got up to her tricks. What happens in my own garden is something I like to keep to myself, and I'm not going to have any kid giving out running reports. If ever people invite Mrs. Peterson and me to go and see them, I feel it's up to me to make a sort of explanation — but that's all, and it comes from the proper quarter. So you can tell this brat's mother what I've told you: to keep her out of my way."

But there was no need to tell Beulah's mother anything, for from the day of Mr. Peterson's visit to the farm, there were no further complaints about her climbing trees.

"I told him to buy a hose," said Aunt Eddie to Wally, when she had summoned him at the end of the week in order to pay his wages. "I knew it would do the trick." She handed him an envelope. "That's what I owe you to date; will you kindly check it?"

Wally checked it, put it into his pocket and nodded his thanks.

"There's a bit of paint needed on the

outside of some of the front windows," he told her. "Care to come and look?"

"Some other time. There's something I want to say to you about the wedding."

"You're calling it off?"

"I am not. It is to take place on Saturday."

To her surprise, his reaction to this news seemed to be one of dissatisfaction.

"Saturday? Why Saturday?" he asked.

"Why not Saturday?"

"Because Thursday'd be better. Thursday's early closing, and all the chaps'll be free and —"

"Chaps?"

"Yes — in the shops. And on the building site. All of them only get off on a Thursday."

Aunt Eddie sat down.

"Perhaps we'd better go further into this," she said. "When I proposed having a few people here after the wedding, I imagined that it would mean a mere matter of —"

"You wouldn't like the church to be full of emptiness, would you? What sort of wedding would that be?" he asked reasonably. "A wedding's when the bride walks in and all heads get screwed round all the way down the pews to see her coming up the aisle. That way, it looks as though she'd got some friends. I sort of mentioned it to the chaps, and gave out a few invitations in the shops. . . . They're all nice chaps. I've never had longer credit anywhere."

"Who else, if I may ask?"

"Well, both Mr. Harveys, of course; I'm hoping one'll be best man and the other'll give away the bride. And I thought it'd be a bit of fun to ask young Beulah and her mother, to see what happened. And Mr. and Mrs. Peterson, to give 'em a change from digging. And there's a couple of truck drivers who —"

"Perhaps we'd better go into numbers. I hadn't quite anticipated —"

"When I was shelling out invitations," acknowledged Wally, "I only thought about filling the church up. I can easily go around telling 'em all to skedaddle when the knot's tied. You don't have to have 'em here."

"I was about to say that I had only anticipated having a dozen or so, but —"

"I can easily say the word when the wedding's over, and they can all go home and then you won't have to —"

"— pollute the woods of Pemberley?"

"Eh?"

"Nothing. Let's get down to numbers."

"That was a quotation, wasn't it? That Pemberley bit."

"It was."

"Then you should let me in on it. I'm all for getting educated — and that's honest. Look at the trouble I take over picture galleries — and I keep reading Shakespeare. Some of it goes over my head, but I like those war bits: 'What, will not this castle yield?' 'The castle is royally manned, my lord, against thy entrance.' "

"You're rattling the ornaments."

"Well, you have to shout a bit at that part. It doesn't sound warlike unless you do. Did you know where that bit came out of?"

"No."

"Neither do I. But it's Shakespeare, so what's the difference? Don't you like all those names: Hotspur and Bolingbroke and Clarence and those? I'd like to be called Hotspur. I, Greta, take thee, Hotspur Booth . . . which reminds me: the wedding. Where were we?"

"I was trying to find out how many people I should cater for. Shall I say thirty?"

"Well, there's no harm in saying, but if one or two long-nosed outsiders cheese their way in, I can't —"

"Sixty. Tea and lemonade."

"Well, I'm grateful and you know it," Wally said frankly, "but don't let's pretend

198

that the chaps wouldn't prefer beer."

"Tea and lemonade."

"Oh, well. . . ."

"And sandwiches and cakes. And a small, very small wedding cake. Dolly will make it."

"Funny world, isn't it?"

"And why?"

"Nothing. I was just thinking that I'd never have thought an old lady in an old house in an old village would feel it worth while spending her dough and her time worrying about getting me legally married. When you first talked about it, I thought the chaps working on the house, or the fellows in the village, would think it funny. But they didn't and they don't. At least, the ones in the village don't; they all thought it was the sort of thing you're always doing. They're used to it."

"I have a reputation for being eccentric. It's very useful at times like this."

He studied her for some moments.

"It's that old business of the lady of the manor, I suppose," he said thoughtfully. "Jellies for the sick and jabs for the sinners."

"It's nothing of the kind. It's simply the feeling that nobody but myself will interest themselves in what happens to Greta or to her child. There may be people who are capable of having a young girl in their employment and caring nothing about her bringing an illegitimate child into the world — but I'm not one of them. You are a casual, careless and probably good-for-nothing young man, and in two or three weeks, when your work here is done, I shall probably never set eyes on either of you again — but there will be in the world a child who owes his name to me. And that seems to me quite sufficient compensation for providing a little light refreshment after your wedding."

She was walking toward the door, and he opened it for her with the slight touch of exaggeration he always added to acts of politeness toward her.

"Pity my Mum can't meet you," he said.

She paused, looking at him in surprise.

"Surely she'll come to your wedding?"

"In spirit — but she can't travel nowadays. Arthritis. She can get on all right in the house or in the garden, but she draws the line at cars or trains or buses. Does her up."

"Well, I'm sorry we shall not see her."

"One day. After the wedding, I'll drive you over — if you'll come. Only a couple of hours each way, and a nice cupper in the kitchen when we get there. If you'd like it."

"I should like it very much. Where did you say she lived?"

"Little place called Greybridge. You go through Exeter. She didn't like the country at first, but now she does. Wouldn't go back to Tooting at any figure. Did I tell you she used to be a nurse?"

"Yes."

"Good nurse, she was. Maternity. She started off by nursing cases in their own homes — that's what started her off with this interest in old houses. She'd have liked to start a nursing home of her own — nothing grand, just three or four rooms — but there wasn't any dough, so she worked in other people's nursing homes till she gave up. Get on well, we do. Only thing we ever disagreed about was that hie-thee-to-an-office stuff."

"When your job with Mr. Harvey is finished," said Aunt Eddie slowly, "why don't you consider taking one here?"

"This house?"

"You could be useful. You're good with your hands, and we need somebody like you."

Wally shook his head.

"It's nice of you," he said, "I can't tell you how nice. But . . . no."

"Why not?"

"Freedom. I've found out that I like to be on my own."

"What are you going to do when you leave here?"

"Maybe I won't leave here. I like this place. I don't say it's a postcard village, but it's got some nice people in it, and a decent little pub, and some nice open country round about — and the sea not too far away. They're building on the other side of Oxterley; I could hang on for a time doing what I'm doing now. The pay's good, and —"

"Is that making a future for your child — or for Greta?"

"I can only work for them. What else?"

"Some kind of permanence. Some kind of home. You'd do well to think over my offer. I won't live forever, and when I do go, this house might be turned into a kind of showplace, so you wouldn't have to turn out; you could still be useful."

"No," he said again. "Don't think I'm not grateful. I am. I can't say much in the way of thank yous, but Greta and I think you're . . . all right."

"Curiously enough, considering all things," said Aunt Eddie, "I think you're

202

all right, too."

"Considering what things?"

"Gossip."

"About me?"

"Yes. But I'm not a fool. I think you're sound enough. If I were pressed, I would say that you weren't as frank as you appear; that is, I think you've got something on your mind that you'd rather keep to yourself. But I don't think it's anything discreditable."

He smiled.

"If you're marrying me off to Greta, shouldn't you check up first?"

"I shouldn't be surprised to learn that Greta has done her own checking up. But perhaps it's as well for you both that I don't believe everything I hear."

"What's the gossip?" he asked.

"That you're new to laboring, for one thing."

"So I am. What else?"

"One or two people seem to think that you tell lies."

"Protection," he said. "Smoke screen."

"If you believe in protection, why weren't you going to extend it to your child?"

"I told you. Bastard isn't a rude word in my dictionary. I don't say that Master Uppercrust, aiming for the top layers of the

Diplomatic Service, doesn't need all his papers in order. But for chaps like me? Never, in all my whole life, did I ever see anybody go up to anybody else in a pub and interrupt the other fellow's mild-and-bitter just to ask if he was strictly legitimate. Who cares? How can I help it if my old man skipped out before the ceremony — which he did. If I'd wanted a passport, I don't say I wouldn't have got onto muddy ground — but all I'm doing after the wedding is taking Greta to one of those boarding houses down by the sea for a couple of nights. Then back to the job. So as I said, who cares?"

"I do."

"You like everything to be legitimate?"

"In every way. The only comfort I get in this world is by realizing that for every one of you, there are a dozen men marrying, sticking to their wives all their lives, doing their best for her, and putting their own interests second and their children's interests first. That way, the world goes round and round, thank God. That's what keeps the pot boiling, and if you get a little scum on top, it doesn't matter."

"Me? The scum?"

"I was speaking figuratively. Why do people like you think that it's easy to keep within the conventions and hard to break out of them? Any fool can break rules. Any silly, empty-headed fool of a girl can sleep with a man, but it takes a smart woman to get him to the altar. And now, if you'll excuse me, I'm going along to see Mr. Waybridge."

"About boiling my pot?"

"About having the wedding on Thursday instead of on Saturday. It'll be at three o'clock; I hope you'll be punctual. And before Thursday, I shall arrange one or two meetings between you and Mr. Waybridge. He will want to ask you a few questions."

He looked apprehensive.

"Catechism and that?"

"Perhaps. He is seeing about the special license."

"How much?"

"It will be my wedding present to you," said Aunt Eddie, and went out.

CHAPTER 8

The day before the wedding was fine and dry; the guests, tomorrow, were to express continuous regret that Wednesday hadn't been the day chosen, instead of Thursday.

It could not be said that anybody was making any special preparations, for only at Tallahouse was there any change in routine; glasses were being taken out and counted, long-disused urns polished. But there was general and genuine interest in the bride and bridegroom; interest, and some speculation. Jendy, ordering buns and bread rolls in large quantities at the baker's, was interested to learn from the comments of other shoppers that Aunt Eddie was by no means the only one who had wanted to see the couple married. Greta was admired, and Wally almost universally liked.

Anabel was away, and would not be back

until the day after the wedding; she had driven up to London — without, Milford told Jendy resentfully in the baker's, so much as a word about why she was going or where she was going to stay.

Beulah gave her own answer to Wally, who was working as industriously and as tirelessly as usual.

"I'm coming to see you getting married," she said. "I bet you'll look funny, getting married in those clothes."

"What makes you think I won't dress up?"

"I heard you tell Jendy."

"Ear to the ground? Haven't you got any business of your own to attend to?"

His tone had lost some of its accustomed casualness; it had almost an edge. She looked at him more closely, but saw nothing to guide her. If she had been older, she would have seen that his face was strained and tense — but she was eight, and the signs escaped her.

"I don't think Greta'll like being married to you," she said.

"No? Who can tell?" he asked. "You'd have to have second sight."

"Well, that's what I have got. Second sight."

He paused and turned to look at her and for the first time in their acquaintance she was aware, with a thrill of triumph, that she had caught his interest. She took a deep breath.

"Nobody's got it; only me," she said.

"You don't even know what second sight is." His voice was contemptuous, but his eyes were watchful. "It's being able to tell what's coming in the future."

"I know it is. An' that's what I can do. I can tell."

"Rot."

Her voice rose.

"I can — so!"

"No, you can't. Only gypsies and witches and people like that have got second sight. I only know one person who's got it. She isn't a witch; she's just an old woman — but she's got it. She can tell you anything that's going to happen in the future. When I want to know anything, I just go and ask her."

"That's not true! If she knew, she'd be able to tell you what's going to happen to you."

"Well, she does know."

"I don't believe you. You're just telling lies. You tell lies all the time."

"So do you — but this isn't a lie. I know

her. But I'm not keen on knowing what's coming, and so I don't ask her much. I only ask her little bits at a time. She won't tell anybody else — only me."

"If she's truly like that, she could get lots and lots of money from everybody."

"She doesn't want lots of money. That's why I don't tell people about her. I wouldn't have told you, only you said you'd got second sight. I keep her a secret, because if I didn't, she'd have queues and queues of people lining up outside her door, and all her nice peace and quiet would be spoiled. — Why don't you take off your mackintosh on a hot day like this?"

"Because it says you mustn't cast a clout till May's out, and May isn't out yet, that's why. I don't believe what you said about the old witch."

"She isn't a witch — I told you."

"I bet she's just made up."

"You'd lose your bet."

"If she was true, you'd be able to say where she lived."

"Well, I can — but it's sort of secret."

"I bet you couldn't tell me, because you're making it up."

He appeared to ponder.

"If you kept to yourself . . ." he brought

out at last.

"Well, of course. What's her name?"

"Her name's Milly."

"Where does she live?"

"Well, when I go to see her, I take the bus from the village — not the local bus, but the one that goes to Exeter. I get off at Exeter and I take a little green bus called Greybridge and District. I get off at Greybridge, which is exactly what it sounds like — a little place with a little grey stone bridge. I cross the bridge, and all by itself in a little patch of trees, there's a little tiny house called Bridge Cottage — and that's where she lives. And it's never any use anybody else going to see her about the future, because I'm the only one she tells it to."

"I bet she'd tell me."

But Wally had turned back to his work, and his interest in the matter appeared to have evaporated. He did not turn again until he heard her moving away — and then he looked after her with a speculative gaze.

"If it works," he murmured to himself, "it works. And if doesn't, the good Lord help her. . . ."

Wally was not the only one that morning

with a look of strain. Allen, studying Jendy when her gaze was elsewhere, thought that she looked pale and out of spirits. She was also unusually silent, and he brought her out of her musing with a quiet question.

"Daydreaming?" he asked.

She turned and smiled at him.

"It's a day for daydreaming," she said.

They were sitting on low cane chairs outside the farmhouse. Even Allen, to whom weather was either hot or cold, wet or dry, had been lured by the unseasonal warmth into a mid-morning break. He was drinking beer. Jendy was cradling a glass of cider in her hands and staring out at the sun-drenched fields.

"Dreaming about what, chiefly?" he asked.

"About Anabel, mostly."

He frowned.

"That's unprofitable, isn't it?"

"I suppose so."

"She's got under your skin, hasn't she?"

"In a way."

"Didn't you . . ." He hesitated, and then went on: "Didn't you ask for it — if you don't mind my saying so?"

"I don't mind. Yes, I suppose I asked for it."

It was true, she reflected. She had imagined

that she could hold her own with Anabel —
and had discovered, painfully, that she
couldn't. It was as simple as that. Anabel
had begun by ignoring her; if she had been
content to be ignored, all would have been
well. But something — in Heaven's name,
what? — had got into her, and she had
decided that it would be amusing to make
her presence felt — just a little. And the
only way of making her presence felt had
been to try and draw some of Roderick's
attention in her own direction. So she had
tried. So she had succeeded. So Anabel had
struck.

Lightly — but the poison remained. The
poison had even spread. From the day on
which Anabel had stopped her and laughed
her devil's laughter, they had exchanged not
a word. But she was aware that wherever she
went on the farm, Anabel watched her —
and she was aware that Anabel was still
laughing.

The poison had spread — for Roderick,
since that day, had been almost ceaselessly
by Anabel's side. The two shared a secret,
and the secret was linked in some way with
Nancy — and that was what came of
challenging Anabel. It was not easy to trace
the cause of the changed atmosphere, but

easy enough to pinpoint the date: the happiness she had felt, the ease, the gaiety, had ended abruptly when Anabel had laughed her out of the game and gathered Roderick to herself.

And there was still Allen — but behind Allen, the other two. On the surface, nothing seemed changed but the fact that Roderick no longer spent part of the days with his brother — but below the surface Jendy could feel tension; tension, and something more frightening than tension: a warning. She was certain that in the other woman's glances, brief and contemptuous though they were, there was something more: something lurking, something waiting. A jungle cat — waiting to spring.

And though men were not credited with intuition, it seemed that Allen was aware of the changed, charged atmosphere. She wondered whether he could feel the derisive waves that flowed from Anabel, feel that they were leaping around Nancy's feet. . . .

"Put it out of your mind," she heard him say.

"Put what out?"

"Whatever's worrying you. Forget it. And if you're worrying about Roderick, don't.

213

He took his eye off Anabel for a time. I almost thought he had it on you — and perhaps she thought so too. So she tightened the rope. Put them both out of your mind, and relax. Be happy. You were, for a time. Relax, and think about the wedding. Wally's being married tomorrow — remember? And I'm going to give away in marriage a girl I never saw in my life until she appeared in a black car with a trailer caravan, however many weeks ago it was."

"Are you still wondering whether Wally's what you called shady?"

"There haven't been any more verbal slip-ups. Perhaps Aunt Eddie's intuition works. All the same, I'm rather sorry I let him blackmail me into allowing him to park the caravan here."

"Blackmail?"

"Of a kind. He's been a bit less full of himself for the past day or two; perhaps the wedding's weighing on him. He's going to lose some of the freedom he talks about."

She did not reply. She was looking at Roderick, who was strolling down from the building site and coming toward them. He stopped before them and stood looking down, hands in pockets, his air thoughtful.

"Funny" — Allen grinned up at him —

"we were just talking about freedom. Wally's. But you seem to have got a day off, too."

"Two days," Roderick said smoothly. "I'm bringing out a drink; want another?"

"Not me." Allen got to his feet and stretched. "Break over — and I shouldn't have had one. You can give Jendy another cider."

He went in the direction of the farm buildings, and Jendy sat watching him. Roderick came out of the house, two glasses in his hands, and took the chair that his brother had vacated.

"Wally tells me you've lent the bride a white dress," he said.

"Given."

"Given the bride. Have you noticed that Wally's looking a bit washed-out?"

"If he prowls all night, it's no wonder."

She was doing all she could to keep her voice pleasant, casual, light — but she knew that her answers were brusque. He had trapped her twice: once into declaring friendship, once into feeling it. She had gone so far as to acknowledge to herself that she liked him — liked his quiet, teasing voice, liked his dark, teasing eyes, his brown, long, thin fingers, his fine head and long, lean

215

figure. She had liked him. The process had been gradual, and she had thought that he had been glad to find her feeling for him losing some of its prejudice.

And then he had allowed himself to be swallowed up by Anabel. . . . The only reason he was here now, with time and leisure to pick up the acquaintance where it had so abruptly been severed, was because Anabel was in London. She would return, and he would go back, she told herself with helpless rage filling her, would go back to his famous comet's-tail act. He didn't look like a poodle on the end of a lead, but what else was he?

He was a cheat — because he had made her believe that he was interested in her, in Allen and Nancy. He had cheated — and worst of all, she was aware that he had known, from the moment of surprising her in tears on the sofa, of her feelings for Allen.

She put her untouched drink on the low table beside her, and rose abruptly. Unfolding himself, he stood beside her, eyebrows raised questioningly.

"You can't go yet."

"I'm sorry — I've got to get home. There's a lot to do."

"Seven minutes," he said.

"Seven . . . ?"

"Seven minutes. I always make a note of the time you manage to bring yourself to spend in my company. It's like taming squirrels; you spend endless time and patience trying to gain their confidence, and just as you think you've done it . . . Swoosh! They've gone. Can't I drive you home?"

"No, thank you. I'd rather walk."

"Then I'll walk with you."

She said nothing; there seemed nothing to say. In silence they walked slowly down to the gate, out of the gate, onto the road.

"Smile," he said suddenly.

She looked up at him.

"Why should I smile?"

"Because somebody ought to. It's Wally's wedding day tomorrow, and nobody's rejoicing — and that's a pity. He isn't rejoicing, for reasons I can't fathom. Last night, he was up at the site for so long that I got up, dressed and followed him — and missed him; he'd gone. If I'd seen him, I was going to ask him what it was all about — but now it'll have to wait until after the wedding. Allen's not rejoicing because he's got his doubts about Wally and doesn't think he ought to be married to Greta until he's been thoroughly screened. You're not rejoicing because you won't take good advice when it's offered to you, and you're still worried about Nancy."

She came to an abrupt stop and turned to face him. For a moment, before she spoke, the peace of the little, lonely country road could be felt — and then she had broken into angry speech.

"What do you know about Nancy, or me, or Allen, or Aunt Eddie — or any of us here?" she demanded. "All you ever did was come down a few times when you probably couldn't think of anywhere else to go. All you ever did was look down your nose at us all. All you ever did was stroll about looking superior, while the rest of us went on our rustic amusements, riding and swimming and going on picnics and camping in one of the fields. You were too bored; too, too bored for words. You came, you yawned — and you went away again, and that was all."

"I must have stayed long enough to gather some pretty accurate impressions," he said coolly. "I knew, for instance, that Nancy was the showy one — and you were the quiet one. I would have bet on her clearing out and your staying on here. Why didn't you?"

"Because —"

She pulled herself up. Whatever she had

been going to tell him was useless. He knew why she had gone away. He knew what she felt about Allen. He knew everything about her. He took no account of veils or disguises or screens; he put them calmly aside and looked at the truth.

The truth. . . .

"Still running away from hard facts?" he asked quietly.

She looked at him. He was strong, clear-cut . . . clear-thinking. He looked, at that moment, oddly gentle — and for one wild moment she trembled on the verge of pouring out to him the story of her years away from Tallahouse; her years in London, keeping away from Allen, keeping away from the look in his eyes whenever they had rested on Nancy. Keeping away from Farhills, in which she would never live as mistress.

There had been nobody to help her. There had been nobody she could tell. Not Allen, not Nancy, not Aunt Eddie. But she knew, standing beside this tall, quiet man, that she could have told him everything. If he had been here.

But she could not tell him now. Something had happened to cut through the ties that were beginning to form between them. Some of the trust she had begun to feel in him had evaporated — and would not return. Not after having seen him in Anabel Druce's arms.

She had come upon them suddenly and — because she was walking on grass — quietly. They had not seen her. She had turned swiftly, gone away silently, and had wondered, then and later and now, why she had been surprised.

He was waiting for her to speak — but she found that she could not. She turned abruptly and went on to Tallahouse, leaving him where he stood.

And it was not until she saw Aunt Eddie's eyes, and the speculation in them, that she realized that she was crying.

CHAPTER 9

The wedding took place in pouring rain.

The rain had begun at daybreak, a light drizzle. By midday the drizzle had turned to light but steady rain — and at a quarter to three, when the guests began to assemble in the little gray church, there was a heavy downpour that had all the appearance of having set in for the rest of the day.

In spite of — in many cases, because of — the inclemency of the weather, guests, invited and uninvited, began to fill the pews. The invitations had been issued by word of mouth only, and there were no ushers, so that there was nobody to question whether old Mrs. Hutton, who sold chickens in the market every other Saturday, was really entitled to a seat in the front row on the bride's side. There was nobody to keep out the picturesque but high-smelling little band of gypsies who for the past two weeks had been encamped down by the river, on Farmer Brewer's land; there was nobody to wonder whether Farmer Brewer himself, seated solidly in the second row with his wife and four children, had ever set eyes on the bride or the bridegroom. It was a wet Thursday afternoon; a wet half-day. There would be no really gripping television until the evening. So Oxterley went to the wedding. The only notable absentees were Anabel Druce, the Petersons and — surprisingly — Beulah.

The most notable absentee of all was the bridegroom.

Greta had entered the church just before the clock struck three, and Wally's wish of having all heads turned to see her entrance was amply fulfilled. She looked beautiful in the dress that Jendy had worn for her Presentation, several years ago; if the bulge in front was not exactly bridal, it was at least a good reason for a wedding. She was on Allen Harvey's arm, and when she had reached the altar and waited for almost ten minutes without there being a sign of the groom, she very sensibly seated herself between Roderick and Allen in the front pew, and composed herself to await his arrival.

"Where the hell's he got to?" Roderick whispered to her.

"He won't be long," Greta assured him. "He had to go and see his Mum."

See his Mum . . . see his Mum . . . see his Mum . . . echoed around the church, and everybody nodded approval. If his Mum couldn't come, a chap had to go and see his Mum; it was only natural.

Wally arrived at twenty past three looking, for the first time in anybody's knowledge of him, almost flustered. Only at the sight of Aunt Eddie's black feathered hat, unseen since the Jubilee of King George the Sixth, did his light-hearted air return. He was dressed in a neat blue suit which, he told Roderick, in an aside, was his office turnout.

Mr. Waybridge was persuaded to come out of the vestry once more, and the ceremony began. The bricklayers, with becoming modesty, had placed themselves in the back rows, leaving the middle pews vacant for the grocer, the baker, the butcher, the milkman and their families. The saddler was there, and the old smith. Old Mrs. Dyer was as usual at the organ, but there was no choir — the choir, average age eight, had gone fishing in Oxterbrook, and so Mrs.

Dyer played a mumbling accompaniment to the wedding and did her best with the Mendelssohn wedding march, and Mr. Tuke the carpenter, who was musical, wished that he had stayed at home and listened to the radio.

There was a little hesitation, after the wedding, as the uninvited debated whether they would or would not follow in the wake of the invited to Tallahouse. It was only tea and lemonade, after all; Miss Latimer wouldn't miss an extra bit of either. So eighty-four people made their way into the Great Hall of the house, and Aunt Eddie ordered Dolly to add cold water to the lemonade and hot water to the tea.

There were no speeches, and the bride and bridegroom left early. The bricklaying contingent went straight to the lounge of the Oxterley Arms and set themselves to wait with as much patience as they could summon for the bar to open. The teetotalers drank up the last of the tea and lemonade and went reluctantly out into the pouring rain. Allen and Roderick were left, and Mr. and Mrs. Waybridge and Milford Druce.

"Why didn't Beulah come to the wedding?" Jendy asked Milford. "I would have thought nothing could have kept her away.

Wally seems to have a sort of fascination for her."

"She didn't say anything about the wedding to me," he answered. "I scarcely saw her this morning. She asked for sandwiches instead of lunch, and took them with her when she went out after breakfast."

"Sandwiches — on a day like this!"

"It seemed odd — but I never like to ask her what she's doing, Jendy dear — let alone why she's doing it. Did you notice the way the light caught Greta's hair as she came in? It was really rather striking. And the flowers . . . who thought of having them all white?"

"Aunt Eddie."

"It was a nice touch; very, very nice. It was a pity the vases weren't deeper. If you had asked me, I could have lent you my largest ones — but never mind; everything went off very well."

Aunt Eddie was of the same opinion, but did not express it until the last guest had gone, and the last volunteer had helped to wash plates and glasses and been dismissed with thanks.

"That's that," she said. "He's married, and I wash my hands of him. Dolly — where's Dolly? I want my dinner."

As they finished dinner, there was a

telephone message from Milford: Beulah had not returned to Gannets for her supper, and he would like to know whether anybody had seen her.

Nobody at Tallahouse had seen her. As the evening wore on, it was learned by degrees that nobody had seen her since morning. She had been seen walking toward the village just after nine o'clock; since that time, nothing had been seen or heard of her.

Inquiries began slowly, for it was some time before Milford Druce could recover from the first overwhelming sense of relief that her absence brought. She was gone; it was almost too good to be true. There was nothing to worry about; nothing. She had simply decided to go up to London and join her mother. She did things of that kind, without a by-your-leave. There was no possible reason for allowing oneself to become alarmed.

But Anabel, reached with difficulty after two hours' telephoning, knew nothing of her daughter.

Even after that, anxiety set in only gradually. Nothing brought home to Jendy the fact of Beulah's universal unpopularity so much as the apathy with which the news of her absence was received in the village.

226

The people of Oxterley were on the whole kindly, with the normal amount of family feeling. They would have been aghast to hear that an eight-year-old child was missing from her home at eleven o'clock on one of the worst nights of the spring, with rain coming down in torrents and a wind that was rough and cold. Any other eight-year-old child. But Beulah's fat, smug, sullen countenance seemed to rise and sneer at sympathy or alarm. Everybody had reasons to bring forward to explain her nonappearance: she was sheltering somewhere; she was with friends whose telephones had been put out of action by the gale and who in consequence were unable to get in touch with her home. There was even a suggestion that she had staged a disappearance in order to draw attention away from Wally and focus it on herself.

But as midnight drew near, search parties were formed under Allen's direction and set off, one by one, and disappeared behind the curtains of rain. The district was divided, areas allocated.

Roderick and Allen elected to search the farm; it was here that it was thought most likely that Beulah would be found. She knew the place well, and it was still felt that she might be sheltering from the storm. Allen chose his men, separated them into two groups and kept one; the other was to work under Roderick's direction.

"We'll take the lower half," he said. "Roderick, you can spread your fellows out along. . . . Jendy," he paused to ask in anger, "What d'you think you're doing here?"

"I walked along the road from Tallahouse," she said slowly, "looking along the road, just to see. . . ."

There was silence. Her words brought her hearers face to face, for the first time, with the more serious possibilities. There was still no thought of abduction — who, in their senses, would saddle themselves with Beulah? — but there were other things to consider. Accidents could happen . . . did happen . . .

"Let me come with you," she begged Allen. "I've got rubber boots and a thick mac and a torch and I . . . I promise I won't get in your way."

"Come on," Allen said.

Their first search yielded nothing. The two parties, wet, mud-spattered, met at the appointed place near the house and exchanged reports: nothing. The place had been combed: nothing. The caravan, shuttered and locked, had been forced open to see if Beulah had hidden herself inside: nothing.

There was nothing to be gained by going over the same ground twice. Allen dismissed the men, and they trudged off in the direction of the village to offer their services to other search parties.

At midnight, Milford made a somewhat hysterical report to the police: his niece was missing.

And just after midnight, Roderick had an idea, and broached it to his brother.

"How about searching the site?" he asked.

"We went there. There was nothing to be seen," Allen told him.

"Where did you look?"

"We started at the top and worked down."

"Did you go as far as Peterson's boundary?"

"We didn't go down to it; we could see it from . . ." He stopped, staring at Roderick. "You're not suggesting that Peterson . . ."

"I'm not suggesting anything. But Peterson wasn't at the wedding. Neither was Beulah. There's just a chance that she went up there and . . ."

They thought of Mr. Peterson and his

strong, coarse hands. Jendy was the first to speak.

"He couldn't do anything to her," she said. "At the moment, everybody in the village is too busy searching to have time to sit down and think — but when they do, every one of them would remember that he'd threatened her. He couldn't — he wouldn't risk it."

"Probably not," Allen said. "But if she did go up a tree this afternoon, and he saw her . . . or if he'd laid a trap . . ."

They said no more. All three had turned in the direction of Roderick's house. They went at a half-run, slipping, slithering, their torches weaving a fantastic pattern of light on the soaked ground before their feet.

They seemed to part instinctively, like animals rounding up a quarry. Jendy was left behind; Allen went to the slope beyond which Beulah had spent so many hours.

And then a smothered sound — a shout — came back to Jendy for a moment before being torn away by the wind. She began to run in the direction from which it had come, and saw Allen closing in swiftly on the other side.

They met, and stumbled on together until they found Roderick.

He was standing some way below them, on the level of the road. Around him were untidy heaps of building materials, lying piled as they had been tipped from trucks. And in the midst of the piles of stone, cunningly hidden, was Wally's small, shabby black car. Roderick was standing beside it, staring at something lying on the seat beside the driver's.

Beulah's brown mackintosh.

CHAPTER 10

Jendy did not kow how long they stood there. She did not remember, afterward, whether anybody had spoken; she recalled only that her own mind, with supreme disregard for the evidence of her eyes, held nothing but stark unbelief. It was Beulah's mackintosh. It was in Wally's car — but it meant nothing. Nothing that could be brought home to Wally.

But she remembered the sudden tensing of Roderick's body, and the speed with which he had suddenly plunged toward the hedge — with Allen and herself behind him. Most clearly of all she remembered the sound that had come to their ears.

A small sound. The cracking of twigs. A moment earlier, it would have been impossible to hear it — but the rain had stopped with a suddenness that had the quality of a roar — and out of the heavy stillness had come the sound of movement in the hedge.

Allen gave a shout — and on the instant, a figure sprang out from the hedge and fled — away, down the slope, across the clearing and down again toward the farmhouse.

In different circumstances, Wally might have eluded them. He was younger than Allen or Roderick — younger and swifter. But he was running in the dark. Their torches kept him in view, but did not illumine the path along which he was speeding. He stumbled, recovered, fell and was up again — but the distance had shortened, and shortened again.

Roderick caught him as he passed the farmhouse. He seized him, swung him around, and for some moments there was no sound but that of heavy breathing. Jendy, coming up with Allen, could hear her heart pumping wildly.

Allen spoke first.

"Talk," he said to Wally. "Talk, and talk fast."

"Talk?" Wally had got his breath back, but his tone held nothing more than irritation. "Talk? You ruddy well nearly —"

Allen hit him, and he went down — and stayed down. From a full-length position he struggled to a sitting one; then he pulled a handkerchief from the jeans he was wearing, held it to his nose and brought it away to examine it in the light that streamed from the windows of the house.

"Blood!" he said. "See what you've done?"

"Get up," directed Allen.

"Not me. Oh no, not me," Wally said firmly. "You go'n take your exercise in a gym. They give you balls to punch."

"Get up," Allen said again. "Get up — and talk."

"If I get up, will you keep your hands off me?"

"If I can."

Wally rose slowly, his handkerchief to his nose.

"What's the big idea?" he asked resentfully. "And how the hell did you know where I was? And if you knew, why the hell did you go and shout? You might have boshed the whole thing up."

"Where's Beulah?" Allen asked. "Come on — where is she?"

"*Beulah?*" Wally's tone was blank with astonishment. "Why bring her up? She's —"

"Your car's down there — very cunningly hidden. And her mackintosh is in it. Now,

234

as I said before — talk."

Wally seemed to be trying to frame a sentence, but his mouth hung open in bewilderment.

"I don't get this," he said slowly at last. "You're not . . . you're not looking for *Beulah?*"

"She's missing. There are search parties out now, all over the place. And your car's hidden, and her mackintosh is in it."

Allen's voice had lost some of its authority. If Wally was acting, it was a performance of outstanding merit. It was some time before he could gather breath enough to speak.

"Well!" he brought out at last. "Now I can die happy. You thought I . . . you were looking . . . you thought . . . *Beulah! Beulah!* Of all the . . . Look. If ever I take to kidnapping, the kid won't be Beulah. Beulah's all right, and nobody's waltzed off with her, you ought to be sorry to hear. Beulah got on the Exeter bus this morning and drove Miller — that's the driver chap who lives in the village — half potty with her questions all the two hours of the way. He . . ." Wally's voice trailed away, and then he put a bewildered question. "But Miller knew. Miller ought to have got back here before six. He could have told you. I saw him when I picked Beulah up at Exeter, and told him to spread the glad tidings that she'd be home in the morning. Why didn't he?"

"One reason would be," Allen told him, "that the Exeter bus left the road — skidded in the mud — fifteen miles out of Exeter on the way back. The driver's waiting there to bring it back. Now you can tell us why you were hiding in the hedge — and why you ran when you saw us."

"I didn't see you — until I ran. I heard you. There was a shout, and suddenly the rain had stopped and sounds were beginning to travel — and I had to get you away. I . . . Look, this is a long story. Do I have to stand out here and tell it?"

They went inside. Allen poured drinks and handed them around; then he telephoned to Milford Druce and to the village.

"Have you called off the posses?" Wally asked him on his return.

"Yes."

They stood for a moment looking at one another and taking in the signs of their night in the mud and the rain.

"You look as though you'd been lying in mud all night," Roderick told Wally. "Now you can tell us what you were doing —

tonight, and all the other nights."

"Other nights? You saw me?"

"I did. But I didn't tell my brother because I was afraid he'd kick you off the place — before I had a chance to find out what you were up to. What were you up to?"

"You mean you've no idea? You mean the only reason you caught me tonight was because you went looking for Beulah?"

"That's all," said Roderick.

"Then that's what called the hand of Fate," Wally said. "Can't we sit down?"

They sat down. Wally sat facing the other three, and they saw that his face, besides being mud-streaked and bloody, was gray with weariness.

"I told you it was a long story," he began. "It's a rum story, too — but it's all true, and when you've heard it, you can take me down to the police and I'll tell it to them and they can take care of all the rest of it.

"It starts off with my job — that job I had in an office. Remember I told you my boss was doing a stretch for embezzlement? Well, we begin there. I'd been with the firm just under, just over a year — can't remember which, at this moment. I was in this little room off the main office — sort of partitioned off — and I had my little canary. And one day, there were the police — not uniformed bobbies, not at that stage, but quiet-looking chaps asking questions and looking into things.

"That was the end of the job. It folded. The day they told me I could go — without my two weeks' pay I was due — I explained that my canary was in my room. Perhaps they thought I was trying to be funny — all they said was that I could go, and fast, and they'd look after the canary. So naturally, that night I went back for it. Nobody'd thought of asking me for the key of my door — which opened into the main corridor. So there I was, unhooking my canary's cage — and I was just going to step out into the corridor again when the elevator stopped — and I got back into the room, quick. I wasn't doing any harm, but somebody might think I wasn't doing any good — so I switched off the light and waited. And then I heard voices, and recognized them as belonging to the boss's brother — and the boss's brother's wife.

"He was a kind of sleeping partner — or something. He'd been out east and had come home a month or two earlier, and he and his wife had been into the office once or twice — they hadn't seen me, but I'd heard them first, and I'd caught sight of them later. I didn't know anything about anything, being a sort of Grade Four employee, but I'd heard the other chaps saying that the two brothers and the wife didn't in their little nests agree. Perhaps brother-from-the-East was finding out things. Perhaps that's what made my boss hurry up and put the dough where the police — and brother — would never be able to find it.

"Well, they went into the office, and I was just creeping out into the corridor again, when I heard some things that, as you might say, rooted me to the spot. I couldn't have moved even if I'd heard the two of them coming toward my other door — the one leading into the office. I just froze there — and listened.

"She was doing most of the talking. She was telling him that the money'd got to be somewhere in a place both the brothers must have known about. The brother in jug, she pointed out, wouldn't have walked into just any old field and dug a hole and buried the loot. He would have picked a place he *knew* wouldn't be tampered with.

"And then she put him through a sort of third degree. Where, where, where had they lived in the past?

"Well, in several places — but none of them seemed likely hideouts for thirty thousand quid. She'd almost given up when he remembered something important. Once, when they were boys, they'd stayed at this —"

"Ravenscroft," brought out Allen slowly. "My God!"

"Ravenscroft," Wally said. "He nearly didn't get it. He tried Croft and Crow's nest and Eagle and then he hit it: this place called Ravenscroft, in a village called Oxterley in Devon. There, in that garden which nobody had ever looked after, they'd played cops and robbers in the undergrowth.

"And so they arranged to go there. And so did I."

"You followed them?" Allen asked.

"Yes. I was out of a job, and two weeks' pay was in the money that was missing. And it was the first time I'd ever run across a bit of information that wasn't available to the general public, and I liked the idea of keeping it to myself — for a time. I didn't think it'd turn out dangerous, with people punching me on the nose."

"Why didn't you go to the police?" Roderick asked.

"Because it sounded a silly yarn — at that

stage. I talked to Greta, and I got hold of a caravan, and we came down here — just to take a look. And then what? Everything in my lap. It was too easy. No sleuth, in the history of sleuthing, ever had it easier. There were the tenants, already in. There was a job for me, in a place where I could keep an eye. There was the news, straight from the horse Beulah's mouth, that digging operations had begun. All I had to do was wait till they located the dough — if they located the dough — and go to the police and tell them about my two weeks' pay.

"And then things began to gum up a bit. Beulah had to be stopped from spying. Well, at last it looked as though she'd stopped — and that's where I made my big mistake. She hadn't stopped. The night before my wedding, I discovered why she wasn't climbing trees any more: she'd discovered the hole I'd made in the hedge, and she was busy trying to burrow her way right through into their garden.

"I'd hacked the hole almost through — but not quite. I took it to all but a foot. Then I'd crawl in, curl up, and I could see next door — and hear next door. And just after I'd found out that Beulah'd been at work on the hole, I found out something else: the dough had been uncovered. It was there — and they'd found it.

"And if Beulah went through that hedge . . . There wouldn't be another drink, would there?"

"Here," said Allen.

"Thanks." Wally drank deep and resumed his tale.

"I was scared — see? Everything would be all right — if only Beulah could be got out of the way. I'd tip off the police, take 'em down to the hedge, and as soon as the dough was lifted out, we'd all break through — me with the police behind me. What? Will not this castle yield?

"So I had to think. If Beulah showed her face, or any other part of her to the Petersons again, she'd be in for it. A chap like him doesn't play games with little girls when they get in the way of him putting his hands on thirty thousand quid. I'd heard some of the things he'd told his wife he'd do to Beulah, and I believed he'd do 'em. So I had to get her out of the way while I watched the last act — and I did it by spinning her a yarn about my Mum being a sort of witch who'd got second sight. My Mum hasn't even got first sight without strong glasses, but Beulah saw a chance to show me up as a liar at last

— and when I saw she was hooked, I gave her the address and travel instructions, and I drove out to the main road on my wedding morning and sure enough, there she was in the Exeter bus, off to see the wizard — I mean the witch. That meant that I had to get to my Mum and tell her the story. But no phone, and no way of sending a message as complicated as this one — so Greta said I'd have to go over and explain what it was all about, and tell Mum that whatever happened, she was to keep Beulah there for the night. I picked Beulah up off the Exeter bus and drove her the rest of the way to my Mum's — and I took Miller aside and gave him a message to bring back here. And all that made me late for my wedding. After the wedding, I drove Greta halfway to Exeter and she finished the journey by bus, so that made two at Mum's for the night. And I came back here and crawled into that hole and lay there watching those two slithering in the mud, dig, dig, digging away to fetch up my two weeks' pay. And it was coming — it was coming up, slowly, slowly, and I was preparing to run for the police, when what happens? Somebody goes and gives a yell. I couldn't believe my ears — but I knew I'd have to get you away from that boundary hedge before the Petersons knew that anybody was around. So I did. And all I got was a punch on the nose. It's still bleeding — see?"

He got to his feet, and the others rose and stood looking at him as he studied Allen and Roderick in turn.

"You," he said to Allen at last, "you'd better be the one to come to the police with me. You're a householder, and you're known here, and you're a good, solid, weighty citizen. Will you come?"

Allen was already in the hall, on his way to the front door.

"Take Jendy home," he called to Roderick. "And then you'd better come down to the village."

They went outside. The clouds had parted, and a watery moon lit a watery scene. Rivulets bubbled past the front door and lost themselves in the puddles in the yard; the orchard was a silvery lake. Wally climbed into Allen's car and they drove away — and then Roderick led Jendy back into the house.

"If you don't need another drink," he said, "I do."

They did not sit down. He poured himself a drink; she refused one for herself, and watched him as he drank.

"Tired?" he asked.

"No. I'm only sorry, in a way, not to see the end. Not that I want to be there when the Petersons —"

"You'll hear about it in the morning — and in the meantime we can go and tell Aunt Eddie what's been going on. And in the morning, too, we'll ask Wally about a few other little mysteries — but I don't doubt he'll have an answer for them all."

She turned toward the door, and he opened it for her. But as she went out, he caught her arm gently.

"Jendy —"

"Yes?"

"Nothing. Only . . . this."

She was in his arms. She thought that he had been gentle, but she knew that he was holding her with a strength that would have prevented her from moving — if she had wanted to.

If she had wanted to . . .

His lips were on hers, and she refused to think — of anything. She was in his arms, and she was at peace, and she could tell herself that this was nothing more than a natural end to the excitement and the activity of the night. This was a release of tension. This was Roderick's way — a good way —

of bringing a fantastic night to a fantastic close.

Neither of them heard the approach of a car. Neither of them heard it stop outside. They did not hear footsteps. It was not until the footsteps stopped close to them that they parted slowly — and turned to find Anabel Druce's blazing eyes on them.

There was a moment's dead silence.

"Finished?" she asked, and the question was addressed to Jendy. "Or haven't you begun?"

"Take me home, Roderick," Jendy said.

"He will. But not yet," Anabel said, and her voice burned with hatred. "You'll hear what I've got to say first. You'd have heard it before if I hadn't been a —"

"Shut up, Anabel," broke in Roderick quietly.

"Not any more. Oh no, not any more! I was a fool not to have said it before. My God! If there's one thing I hate, it's hypocrisy! When I look at this hands-off character, and think of her sister —"

Jendy made an attempt to pass, but the other woman blocked her way.

"It won't take long," she said, "and you'll hear it, even if I have to scream it out loud while Roderick tries to stop me. It's this: I went to London to check, but I was sure before. And I'm willing to bet you were sure, too — but innocence was always your line. Don't tell me that you didn't know what Nancy was doing in Seville. She wasn't with the Navarretes. She was with Carlos Navarrette. She —"

Jenny made a swift movement to try and get past, but this time it was Roderick who put out a hand and grasped her arm. Drawing her to him, he held her and spoke quietly.

"Hear it out," he said. "It's the worst way, and it's my fault, but . . . hear it out."

"Yes, hear it out," jeered Anabel. "And don't tell me it's news to you — except the last bit. Nancy was living with Carlos Navarrete before she came back here. She went back because she found Allen pretty slow going after Carlos and his crew. She met him in Madrid and he took her down to Seville — the way he took me down, and others before me. And a week ago, he left her — the way he left me. And good luck to him. You don't hold a man like Carlos Navarrete for long — but what makes me laugh is to think of Nancy, Nancy Marsh the unattainable, taking on Carlos after I'd done with him! It ought to teach you, and teach her to keep your feet on the ground. You both belong with the rest of us, and —"

But Jendy had torn her arm from Roderick's hold and was running down the corridor, across the hall, out of the house. Behind her was the laughter that had haunted her for so long — but now she knew why Anabel was laughing.

Somewhere on the road to Tallahouse, in the faint light that may have been the moon or may have been the dawn, she heard Roderick's car stop beside her, felt his hand drawing her in beside him. They spoke no word, either then or when he left her at the door of the house. He seemed to sense that she was no longer near enough to be able to hear what he said.

She knew that Aunt Eddie was in her room, watching her silently as she went swiftly, feverishly about her preparations. She was aware that things were handed to her, and she took them, and put them away. . . .

The village awoke to the sensation of the arrest of the Petersons. A small crowd watched the police cars drive away, and Oxterley was left to talk over the greatest excitement it had known for years.

But by that time, Jendy was thirty thousand feet up, airborne, on her way to Nancy.

CHAPTER 11

She flew to Madrid, and drove straight to Nancy's studio, to find it closed and shuttered. She went on to Seville by train, took a room at a hotel — and made her way to the palace of the Navarretes.

Her first visit proved futile. Nobody, she was told, was at home. No, there was no English lady. There was nobody.

She tried again — that day and the next — and the next. And it was then that she encountered the little boy with huge brown eyes and the enchanting smile, and understood from his gestures that he wished her to follow him.

He led her through a maze of streets, narrow and narrower, and then, understanding that the sun was too warm and her heels too high, signaled a taxi and put her into it, taking his own place by the driver.

They got out in a little flower-enclosed plaza, and the taxi was told to wait, and the little boy led her to a tall doorway that opened on to a cool, half-hidden courtyard.

A white staircase curved up to a wide white landing. And at one of the doors, the little boy stopped and pointed. Jendy knocked — and the door opened and Nancy stood before her.

There seemed no need for words. The two met — and the last few weeks fell away. There seemed nothing, at first, to say; nothing to do but thank the little boy, pay the little boy and send him smiling away.

"This is a sort of hotel," Nancy said, as they stood looking at one another. "I came here when Carlos left me."

It was said — in one sentence.

"I should have known — but I didn't," Jendy said. "Why didn't you tell me?"

"How could I? It was one thing to live with a man. It was another thing to live with a man who'd run through half a hundred women — the last of them Anabel Druce. It was one thing to live with a man because you loved him; it was another thing to be drawn back to a man you didn't love, simply because you wanted something that he could satisfy and Allen couldn't satisfy. How could you have understood?"

"I could have helped, perhaps. I could have . . . been around while you got over it."

"I thought of that — but I decided I'd have to work it out for myself. There were two lives. One was there, with Allen. The other was here — with or without Carlos. It seemed to me that I'd been happy here, and could be happy here again. So I came back — and as soon as I'd left England, I knew I'd thrown away everything."

"Then why —"

"I came down here with Carlos, but it was dead. And that was the worst part: trying to find out what I'd really wanted. I knew I'd lost my bearings — and that isn't . . . it isn't a pleasant feeling. I was frightened, for a time — and then I realized that you have to choose, and if you choose wrongly, there's nothing you can do about it."

"Come back with me."

"No." Nancy's voice was quiet. "No. I shan't come back — ever. Not to Oxterley. There are some things you can't rebuild. I've thought about it till I can't think about it any more — and I know that when I left Allen, I did something I — I can't undo."

"Come back to London with me."

"No. I'd have to see Aunt Eddie — and there'd be nothing to say. She'll never forgive me for leaving Allen."

"But" — Jendy's voice was urgent — "apart from Allen, there are so many things! Tallahouse is your home. You loved it. You always . . . Don't you remember how happy we were there when we were young?"

"Yes, I remember."

"Then . . . *that's* still there."

Nancy was at the window, staring out as she had stared out on the morning she had come to the Mews flat . . . how long ago? Her back was to Jendy, and she did not turn as Jendy put a desperate question.

"Nancy — don't you want to come back, ever?"

She could see, beyond Nancy, all that was outside: beauty, color, warmth, all that had charmed and dazzled the artist's eye. The garden shimmered in the heat.

"Don't you want to come back — ever?" she asked again.

And then Nancy turned and faced her, ashen-faced and with a look of bitter hopelessness in her eyes.

"I'd give my soul," she said slowly.

Jendy, trembling, spoke with what steadiness she could.

"Then . . ."

"Go away, Jendy — *please.* . . ." It was an appeal not to be refused. "Go away — go back, and leave me alone. I can't bear it — not yet. Please, *please* go. . . ."

Jendy turned and went blindly out of the room. She went downstairs and, through a mist, saw the taxi and got into it. She leaned back against the cushions, her limbs shaking.

She got her key from the desk and went up to her room. Only in the cool dimness of the corridor did she feel the tears that poured down her face. She stood before the door of her room struggling to insert the key in the lock.

And then a hand — a man's hand — took the key from her and opened the door. An arm came around her shoulders and urged her gently inside. She heard the door close.

Into her hand Roderick put a large, clean white handkerchief.

"I've got another one if you need it," he said.

CHAPTER 12

"But I don't see —" began Jendy for the twentieth time.

"Quiet," said Roderick. "Why do women talk so much? I'm trying to explain things to you in decent order, and you keep breaking in. Lean back and just let me drive and tell you in my own way — and in my own time."

"Where are we?" she asked.

"You may well ask. You've shown no sign of being anywhere up to now. We're about thirty kilometers south of a place called Caceres, on the way to Salamanca, Valladolid, Burgos, San Sebastian and places north. We're not hurrying, as you observe. When I say observe, I speak figuratively, because you haven't observed one single point on the landscape since we left Seville. I feel —"

"But —"

"— that however painful the circumstances

which brought you to Spain, your mind is now sufficiently at rest to allow you to make the most of your return trip. But I dare say you're now busy wondering what Aunt Eddie'll say about your cruising round with me, unchaperoned. I'm glad to note that you've stopped crying. Do you know that you're the only woman I've ever driven in this part of the world who couldn't appreciate the Roman theater at Merida? But you hadn't stopped crying then. I'm rather sorry I didn't decide to stay another night there — but you'd only have spent it as you did the other one, weeping in your room."

"Roderick, do please answer my questions."

"Only if you're ready to put them sensibly and consecutively and listen dry-eyed to the answers."

"All right. Why did you come?"

"I've told you. To take you home. Why didn't I come out by air, like you? Allen was crazy to fly out, but I got him, finally, to agree to driving out with me. It gave you time to talk to Nancy; it gave me time to talk to Allen. There was a lot to be said — by everybody — before we met."

"Who told Allen?"

"I did. There's a time for not telling and

a time for telling, and the time for telling had arrived. So I talked."

"Did you tell him everything?"

"I think so. I told him things that nobody but myself could have told him: notably, that Nancy merely fell under the same spell as I did. When you meet people like the Navarretes, you stop thinking rationally. They put you — I'm sorry to repeat the term, but it explains it better than any other — under a spell. You lose, for a time, the power to think clearly. You're so dazzled that you can only see the brightness; everything around it is obscured. Then the spell breaks, or you get used to the light, and you begin to see the surroundings. I never imagined, when I brought Nancy into the circle, that she'd be in any danger. She was going back, eventually, to marry Allen; she told me so. I knew, of course, how potent Milagros was, but — being a man — I didn't realize that Carlos would have the same devastating effect on a woman. Perhaps I was so glad to be able to meet Milagros, at last, without feeling anything at all, that I was willing to believe that all she and her brother would do would be to draw Nancy into the circle that so few foreigners could enter. Everybody interesting, everybody artistic or well known moved in or around the Navarrete set. I wanted Nancy to widen her knowledge, widen her experience . . . but not to the extent she did."

"When she got engaged to Allen, and then said she wouldn't marry him, and came back to Spain, did you —"

"— realize what had happened? No. That is, I thought she'd merely lost her head, as I'd once lost mine. I didn't tie Carlos into it until you told me that she was staying with the Navarretes in Seville. I knew that Milagros was in London — Anabel had met her there, so what you said made me uneasy. I rang up friends of mine in London, and learned that Nancy was with Carlos in Seville — and learned from Anabel that Nancy and Carlos had been living together in Madrid. If I'd had your gift for weeping, I'd have wept then. I wanted to go to Allen and tell him the whole story — but there you were, complicating things. If I told him, I was pretty sure I knew what he'd do; what in fact he did do: go straight out to her. But there were other considerations."

"What other considerations?"

"Several. If I hadn't — like Nancy — taken the wrong decision once, I'd probably have had more confidence in my ability to size up the situation. But I hesitated; I wondered if, after all, I knew Allen as well as I thought I did. If I told him the truth about Nancy, would he go out to her — or would he decide to put her out of his mind? And if he put her out of his mind, would he fill the space with another woman? Do you read Jane Austen? Do you remember what she gave as the reason for Henry Tilney's falling in love with Catherine Morland? I'll quote: . . . 'A persuasion of her partiality for him had been the only cause of his giving her a serious thought.' Worse still, 'His affection for her originated in nothing better than gratitude.' It was a terrible risk. There you were, imagining yourself in love with Allen and —"

"Imagining? For eight years?"

"Don't start crying again. It was nearer nine. You weren't much more than sixteen when I came back to Farhills and saw your faithful little heart in your eyes every time you looked at him. I didn't dream it would cling for so many years and survive his engagement to Nancy — but I understood, when I got to know you, that once your affections were engaged, so to speak, you wouldn't see anything you didn't want to see. Witness your obstinacy in the fact of the evidence piling up against Nancy."

"I didn't —"

"— show your feelings about Allen? Not to Nancy or to Aunt Eddie or to him. I dare say not. But when I walked into the room that evening and saw you crumpled up on the sofa, crying your heart out, and saw the look in your eyes when I told you that Allen was coming in, I marveled. All those years . . ."

"You don't stop loving people just because —"

"— just because they happen to be in love with someone else? Unfortunately not. What you can do is grow out of a girlish infatuation and survey the landscape in order to pick out another candidate on whom you can fix your attention. But surveying the landscape, as I've found out since I brought you away from Seville, isn't one of your habits. Will you please note that Caceres, which we shall reach shortly, was founded in 54 B.C. by a gentleman named Quintus Cecilius Metelus. It was taken by the Arabs in the ninth century and reconquered no less than four times by Christian kings. The old town is surrounded by Roman walls and . . . By our Lady of Dolors, you're not crying *again?*"

"N-no. When did Allen tell you he was

coming out to Nancy?"

"About three seconds after I'd told him of Nancy's sin-and-shame. He reached for his hat and began looking up the number of B.E.A. All that meekness, all that patience and that resolve to let Providence decide whether she came back to him or didn't come back to him . . . all that went straight out of the window. He became, all at once, an extremely happy man."

"Happy?"

"Of course. He saw that at last there was something he could do something about. Something he could fight. Nobody can argue with a woman when she's handing out all that nebulous stuff that Nancy brought back to England. He can only talk around the thing to a woman who isn't listening anyway. By the time he's thought of one or two rational arguments, she's gone. But when he understands that a girl of Nancy's background and upbringing has got herself into a mess with people Allen regarded, regards and I fear will always regard and refer to as a bunch of dagoes, then he knows exactly what to do: take her by the hair and drag her back to sanity. So we drove out together, not wasting time as you did in Madrid. That's where Carlos was — why would she go there too? So we went to Seville, and to the Navarrettes, and your little boy with the eyes told us where you were, so we drove there — and Allen wanted to go up, but I thought he ought to wait until you'd had your say. And then out you came, too stricken to see us, and climbed into your tumbril and drove away. I left Allen flying up the stairs, and I followed you back to your hotel and if I hadn't let you into your room, you'd still have been standing there, howling, and looking for the keyhole."

"I would have liked to see Nancy again."

"You will — when Allen brings her home. If she'd wanted to see you, she'd have said so — but it'll be a long time before she gets her mind off Allen. I dare say she'll always think of him as a nice noble fellow, whereas all he is, and was, is a sound, sensible man who could have saved her a lot of trouble if only she'd had the sense to put him into the picture from the beginning. But women like drama. She'll remember all her life the way he came into that room. She was standing with her back to him, staring hopelessly out of the window, and she had no idea he was there until —"

"You weren't there. You were with me."

"Don't you ever use your imagination?

How do you think they met? Or do the remnants of your infatuation for him prevent you from thinking about it?"

"Remnants?"

"Dregs. The thing that beats me is why you missed seeing how wrong you would have been for him. It beats me. Everything about him — his quietness, his steadiness, his inclination to go into ruts, his lack of romantic imagination — cried out for a partner like Nancy. You were much, much too steady for him, much too balanced, much too sane. Together, you'd have grown into a dull couple indeed. If only you'd allowed yourself to think, you would have realized that I was the one who needed a woman like you. It'll dawn on you one day, and in the meantime, God grant me patience. And here's Caceres, and I know a place nobody else knows about where they give you *vino fino* that trickles down very, very sweetly. And tomorrow morning we'll get organized: early breakfast, and a tour round the little shops to buy a picnic lunch. Have you any ideas?"

"Bread, cheese, butter. Fruit."

"And a foot or so of that garlic-laced sausage."

"You like it?"

"So will you when you get to know it. I'll buy a knife and a corkscrew and some wine."

"In a wicker basket?"

"If you like." He glanced at her. "That's it. Smile. Be happy. You're on the open road, in a comfortable car, with a reliable escort. Sunny days ahead, warm nights; lunch by the wayside, dinner on a vine-hung terrace. If I see one more tear, I'll stop the car, put you out and find me another woman. A woman, moreover, who doesn't shut herself into her room immediately after dinner and reappear only at breakfast."

She sat looking out at the warm countryside, and presently found peace stealing over her. Roderick drove steadily and, it seemed to her, tirelessly. The wind rushing past lifted her hair, and she got out a scarf and tied it around her head. The open road; ahead, places she had never seen. Perfect weather, and a man beside her who was rather more than a reliable escort: informed, experienced, never at a loss. And patient — and kind.

More than anything, she came to look forward to their midday halts for lunch. Roderick would do nothing but spread a rug and wait. Jendy laid out the food, and then they ate, and he stretched himself, declared

263

himself wine-drugged, and slept. She sat beside him in the shady seclusion, watching the long, strong figure, and grew to understand, in the quiet hour that followed, how much he had done for her in the past weeks. But she had not yet learned all.

"Salamanca next," he told her. "Did you read it up last night, as I told you to?"

"The book you gave me was in Spanish. I didn't follow much of it."

"Population?"

"I skipped that bit. There's a Roman bridge — Puente Romano — over the river."

"Name of river?"

"I don't . . . yes, I do know. The Tormes."

"Correct. Proceed."

"It's two hundred and thirty-four kilometers from Burgos, and two hundred and fourteen kilometers from Caceres."

"About halfway between the two, in fact; that's why I elected to stay there."

"We're not traveling very fast, are we?"

"You want to speed?"

"No. I meant that we seem to spend a lot of time at all the halts."

"You're in a hurry?"

"No, but —"

"You want to see as little as possible of all

these historic cities?"

"No, but —"

"But what?"

"Money. If you'd let them make out separate bills, so that I could —"

"Now *that* illustrates what I was trying to tell you about the unsuitability of you and Allen as a couple. When *they* go home, Nancy'll concentrate on enjoying herself while Allen gets out his little book and jots down what they spent at the last hotel. You and he together would have spent the entire trip adding up columns and wondering whether they overcharged you for the wine. What makes you such a worrying woman?"

"I wasn't worrying."

"You'll grow out of it. After all, I've learned to wait. I've known you, man and boy; watched you go through various phases; watched you —"

"You didn't."

"Didn't what?"

"Watch me. You merely registered — so you say — that I watched Allen. When," she asked curiously, "did you first *see* me?"

His answer was prompt.

"When I found you howling on the sofa. You looked up, and I noticed several interesting things. Want to know?"

"Yes."

"Your eyes, for a start. Wet, but still beautiful. Your silly little nose. The way your hair fell all by itself into its own disorderly order. Your skin, so much more transparent than Nancy's. Other things, too; the fact that you were crying because Nancy had thrown away something you felt she ought to have prized; crying because Allen was hurt. It seemed to me extraordinary that you should have been sitting there shedding tears for two other people."

"Two people I loved."

"Perhaps that was it. Perhaps there was love in that room when I walked in — and I caught it. From that moment, d'you know something? I felt as though I'd *arrived*. I didn't know quite where I'd got to, but I had the peaceful, satisfied feeling one gets after a long, hard walk. I was home. — Funny, wasn't it? Just to fall in love like that."

"You didn't stay in long."

He gave her a sidelong glance.

"Meaning?"

"Meaning that shortly afterward, you were making love to Anabel. I saw you. You —"

She said no more, for he had brought the car to an abrupt halt at the side of the road, switched off the engine and turned to face her.

"You saw me — making love to Anabel? This I must hear."

"She was in your arms. You —"

Once more she stopped — this time because his laughter drowned her speech. He had put his head back and had given way to helpless mirth. Once or twice he tried to stop himself, but each time the laughter rang out again.

"What's funny?" she inquired at last.

"You." Laughter overcame him again. "Oh Jendy, Jendy, you're so . . . Nobody was ever like you."

"Laugh," she invited. "I like to see you happy. But I did see you kissing Anabel Druce."

He was sober now.

"How in the world," he asked slowly, "did you manage to see that? I thought we were out of sight."

"I was going to talk to Wally, and for once, not seeing you or Anabel up there, I went by way of the building site. And I . . ."

"And there we were?"

"Yes. There you were."

He studied her for some time in silence.

267

"And when you saw us," he asked at last, "what did you think? No." He corrected himself. "What did you feel?"

"Surprised — I don't know why."

"What else did you feel?"

"Is it important?"

"Yes, it's important. Quite vitally important, in fact."

"I felt angry."

"Nothing else?"

"I felt . . . humiliated, I think, in some odd way. It seemed to me that you'd spoiled something. Things had been . . . everything had seemed to be going well, and then —"

"And then the illusion was shattered."

"I was never under any illusions about you. From my earliest years, everybody's been only too ready to tell me how different you were from Allen."

"So I am. Did you put me down as a philanderer? Did you think I was . . . You needn't answer, because you didn't think of me at all — until lately. And I wouldn't have held out any hope to myself that you'd ever think about me at all — if you hadn't told me just now that you didn't like my kissing Anabel Druce."

"Kissing? You were holding her in a —"

"Wrong. She was holding me."

"You didn't seem to mind."

"I didn't. I'd succeeded in getting out of her something I wanted very much."

"That's exactly what it looked like."

"And so you wrote me off?"

"No. Somehow . . . I don't know how . . . there seemed to be something wrong with the picture. But how can you ignore the evidence of your own eyes?"

"By working out that if I'd wanted to make love to Anabel, I could have done it, and welcome, any time during the past ten years. By working out that until I heard from you where Nancy was, and learned what Nancy was doing, I'd been finding it quite easy to keep Anabel at arm's length. But after that it became necessary to persuade Anabel to keep her mouth shut, and I did it in the only way I knew would be successful. What I did, I did for you. That embrace was suffered on your behalf. Do you or don't you owe me an apology?"

"I'm sorry. Next time I see you with a beautiful woman in your arms, I'll go straight up and thank you. I'll —"

His lips, resting on hers, checked further speech. Their touch was light and fleeting, and then he drew away and looked at her.

"The first of many," he said gently.

"Jendy, will you marry me when we're both old and gray and when you've had time to absorb the fact that you never, after the impressionable age of sixteen, loved my brother? Will you marry me in the dim and distant future, when I've at last convinced you that what you loved was Farhills? Will you marry me when I've made you at long, long last understand that the happiness you always felt at Farhills had to have a center, a core. So you fixed on Allen. At sixteen, you undoubtedly loved him. And after that, you never stopped to take out your emotions, give them a brisk shake and get the moths out of them. If Allen had shown signs of falling in love with you, you would have been forced to face the problem of whether you wanted him or not — but he loved Nancy, and your feelings, instead of being de-mothed, were laid gently in lavender and kept sweet and fresh. You and Allen had nothing to give one another. You and I have everything. I need you and you need me. I need your stick-in-the-muddiness and you need my more volatile qualities. I the ocean, thou the billow, as the song said, though I could never understand why any girl put up with being called a billow." He bent and kissed her, this time lingeringly. "Will you love me one day, Jendy?"

There was a long, long silence. At the end of it she spoke slowly and thoughtfully.

"Salamanca," she said, "is the capital of the province of the same name and is a bishopric and a famous old university town."

"Just as you say," said Roderick, and drove on.

"Valladolid," she said, two days and some two hundred kilometers later, "is a city of Celtiberian origin. It . . . What's Celtiberian?"

"H'm?"

He was lying on his back, drowsy, content, his eyes on her as she sat with her back against a tree. The remains of their picnic were between them.

"I said, what is Celtiberian? Celtic and Iberian, I suppose."

"Bright girl."

"The cathedral . . . Do you know how much of that sausage you've eaten in the past forty-eight hours?"

"Tell me."

"I bought five, and you've had them all. How do you *do* it?"

"Well, I merely ask the woman sitting next to me to take off the skin and cut it in slices, and I —"

"Do you realize that when we started on this journey, you were going to act as guide? All you've done —"

"We can come back and look at all the cathedrals when we're married. We'll bring the children and shepherd them around and —"

"Can I induce you to keep your mind on facts and not on fantasies?"

He smiled gently at her.

"Frankly, Jendy honey, you can't. I feel so happy lying here looking at you that I can at last understand all those poets who said that they were content to die with their eyes on the beloved object. I'm sorry to refer to you as an object."

"What poets, for instance?"

"Ah! She thinks she's caught me. Well, how about that bit Othello recited? Something about 'If it were now to die 'twere now to be most happy?' That do? Not very well, I suppose. Who can quote after an intake of sun-warmed wine? I can't — unless, of course, I use old Omar Khayyam."

"Why don't you let me drive sometimes?"

"I'll buy you a car to do the shopping in when we're married."

"It's time we went on."

"Where to? Shall we turn and go back to Seville and do it all over again? Shall we, Jendy?"

She hesitated, and he sat up and in a swift movement caught her arm and repeated his question.

"Shall we, Jendy?"

She raised her eyes and met his.

"No," she said. "I don't want to go back. I want to go on."

"With me?"

"Perhaps."

"Are you enjoying yourself?"

She drew a soft, deep breath.

"Enjoying, perhaps, isn't the word," she said.

He seemed satisfied. He released her arm and rose and helped her to her feet.

"It's a funny thing about women," he said, as he carried the picnic hampers to the car and then settled her in and took his place beside her. "You never know what they're really saying until —"

"Until?"

"Until you look into their eyes."

Burgos . . . but not San Sebastian. A change of plan, and a turn northeastward. Logrono, Pamplona and so to the border through Villaba and Larrosoana and on to Roncesvalles. Up and over the Pass.

And so to France. Roderick left her while he completed the frontier formalities, and came back to stand beside her as she sat in the car.

"France, Jendy. No more Spain. No more burned landscapes and burning sun. No more garlic sausage of *that* kind. France, darling Jendy; highly civilized, fair and green and welcoming and gastronomically tempting. And after France, England. Home. Do you want to get home?"

She had no answer to make, and he did not press her. He might, she thought, have read the answer in her eyes.

Home — with Roderick.

CHAPTER 13

"It was a boy," Aunt Eddie said. "Eight pounds six ounces, with eyelashes a yard long."

"When?" asked Jendy.

"Just after Greta came back from his mother's. I told Wally he ought to have gone to fetch her, but he said the police had a few more questions to ask, and so she came by bus. And most fortunately I had a feeling that a bus ride on top of all the other excitement would bring everything on, so I thought I'd just walk down to meet the bus, and so I did. And the moment she got off and saw me, she said: 'Quickly.' "

"Wasn't Wally —"

"He was at the bus stop, naturally — but what use is a man at a time like that? I pushed him aside and took matters into my own hands. She came out of hospital yesterday. Today, they're moving out of Farhills and going to look for a house on the other side of Oxterley. I've picked several out for them to look at."

"He wouldn't stay here?" Jendy asked.

Something went out of Aunt Eddie's face — a light, a glow.

"No. He refused. He could have worked here. I pointed out the advantages of that great garden for a growing child — but he wouldn't stay. He says he wants to be free. Who's free in this world, I'd like to know? He — Who's that driving up?"

"Roderick."

"Oh. Well, I suppose I shall have to get used to it. What does he want?"

Roderick wanted them to go and say goodbye to Greta and Wally.

"The caravan's just down the road," he said. "Greta wants to see Jendy before she goes."

"She isn't going far," commented Aunt Eddie. "I'll come with you."

They went in Roderick's car. Wally and Greta were waiting for them, seated in the little black car. Greta was holding the baby; behind them was the neat little caravan. Wally got out and opened its door.

"Come and see," he invited. "You've

never been inside, and this is your last chance."

"Selling it?" asked Roderick.

"Yes. Chap I know offered me a good price."

They went in one by one: Aunt Eddie, Jendy, Greta, Roderick — and Wally came last to do the honors. Aunt Eddie took the baby and cradled it with awkward gentleness.

"Spick and span, no?" Wally asked with pride. "Sorry to be giving it up, in a way. Never thought I'd be settling so soon. Came here not knowing a soul, and now look: we've won the love'n trust of all. Even if they did think I'd carved up Beulah and hidden her in the hedge. Miss her, in a way — her and her mother. Something seems to've gone out of my life."

"Speaking of trust," Roderick said, "there are one or two points you could clear up for me."

"Name them," Wally invited.

"Why did you say that your mother was dead, and then say that she was a nurse and —"

"Easy," Wally said. "Too easy. My mother *is* dead. Died when I was born — and that, if you want to know, is why I sweated so much when Greta was having this little chap.

My mother turned up at the nursing home my Mum was working in, and my Mum said that from the start, she didn't like the look of it. No marriage lines and no dough and nobody coming forward when she died to say they'd like to have me. And that was where my Mum came in. She took me, and nobody made any fuss and the nursing home was glad to have a kind of awkward situation ironed out so nicely. My Mum took me, and she was the only Mum I ever knew and she was Mum enough — but she always thought I ought to call my mother Mother when I talked about her."

"Didn't you ever learn anything more about her — or about your father?" asked Roderick.

"Only what my Mum heard from my mother in what you might call the chatty intervals of having me. She told my Mum that the picture she gave her was my father."

"Picture?" repeated Roderick.

"The oil-on-canvas sort, same as the ones in that gallery at Tallahouse — but no gilt frame, natch. There he is, over my bunk. I always keep him there. I'm yours, you old buzzard, I say to him every night; I'm yours, even if you did dodge, as we might say, the issue." He picked up the unframed portrait and looked at it thoughtfully. "Not much resemblance, till you look at the eyes — and the mouth. My mother painted it; called herself Luisa and said she came from Brazil. But that made it a bit awkward for Mum when it came to naming me. I couldn't be Luisa, and all she knew about Brazil was that it was where the nuts came from. Monkey nuts? No; I wasn't that ugly. Hazel nuts? For a girl, same like Luisa. So that left walnuts, and I got to be Wally. What those ships are doing behind my Papa, I can't tell you. Maybe he was a seafaring chap — but the ships look like those old tubs that Drake used to drive around in. See? Still, I suppose. . . ."

His voice trailed away. Looking around at his audience he had become aware that something was amiss. Roderick was looking at Jendy, who, white-faced, was staring at Aunt Eddie. Aunt Eddie's face was gray. She was trembling — so much, that Wally moved toward her and held out his arms for the baby.

"Gimme," he said gently. "It's hot in here for you. I'll open . . ."

Once more he stopped. Aunt Eddie, refusing to hand him the baby, was standing looking down at it with tears pouring down her cheeks. But in spite of the trembling and the tears, the voice in which she addressed Wally was firm.

"Your picture," she told him, "would have been hanging in the Tallahouse gallery — if I hadn't allowed your mother to go away without selling it to me after his death. The sketch of the portrait is in my possession at Tallahouse."

There was a silence that seemed to last indefinitely. Nobody seemed to have anything further to say. Then Wally shook himself from what appeared to be a not-too-happy dream.

"The baby," he said, with all the fortitude he could muster, "is going to be called Wally. And —"

"The baby," said Aunt Eddie, "is going to be called Hugh Bertrand Latimer."

"And," proceeded Wally dazedly, "I'm going to find a house in —"

"You and Greta and the baby," Aunt Eddie said, turning toward the door, "are coming home."